SPILLIN

Stephen Moore lives in Newcastle upon Tyne
with his wife, his young son and his cat (the cat
disputes this, and claims that *they* all live with
her). He spent several years happily lost in the
strange old world of museums, working as an
exhibition and graphic designer. Until, that is,
one day he discovered the magic that is
storytelling . . .

SPILLING THE MAGIC is his first novel for
children.

Spilling the Magic

Stephen Moore

Hodder
Children's
Books

a division of Hodder Headline plc

A Catalogue record for this book is available
from the British Library

ISBN 0-340-66098-8

Typeset by Avon Dataset Ltd, Bidford-on-Avon

Printed and bound in Great Britain by
Cox & Wyman, Reading, Berks

Hodder and Stoughton
A division of Hodder Headline plc
338 Euston Road
London NW1 3BH

For Helen Carol Moore

CONTENTS

– ONE –

The Stringers

Want to know a secret, a big'un? Well, do you?
I was never much good at keeping secrets. Not
whoppers like this.

What can I possibly know worth telling, I
can almost see you thinking? Well, I know . . . I
know that pigs *can* fly. I know that *real*
dragons are vegetarians. I know that lots of
things aren't what they seem to be, and that
proper magic works. And, I know that you can
help save a whole world from being snuffed
out to nothing, without even knowing that
you're doing it.

Yeah, go on – laugh. Daft fairytale stuff. Well,
do you know something? I couldn't care less
whether you believe me or not. And if you're
still interested you're just going to have to get
on with it. Start right at the beginning. The
summer before last, the day I was sent with my
sister, Mary to stay with *The Stringers*.

You see, if we hadn't been sent to stay with

the Stringers, there would have been nothing to tell . . .

It was a stinking hot morning. The kind that sends buckets of sweat dribbling down the inside of your shirt. And the air was too thick to breathe. I had to chop it up into little bits and suck it between my teeth just to swallow it. Well, nearly.

The rotten bus had dropped us off at the bottom of Lemington Hill. We – Mary and me – we wanted to be at the top of the hill. Some holiday this was going to be.

'I still don't see why they couldn't have taken us with them,' Mary said. She was sulking. She had been sulking ever since leaving home. I swear, if I hadn't picked up my suitcase and walked away, I would have thumped her.

'I don't want to hear it again, Mary,' I said, and attacked the hill with giant steps. Row after row of tiny red-brick houses and grubby little corner shops crammed the hillside. I thought somebody had accidentally dropped them there and just not bothered to pick them up again. Windows and doors were slung open all

2

over the place – it was so hot even the buildings were panting for breath.

Dad had said their holiday was a sort of second honeymoon – for Mam. 'You know Billy, after *her bother* and *the hospital* and that.' He had given me one of his knowing looks that was meant to explain everything, but didn't. 'The Stringers are canny enough. And you won't mind not going with us just this once – *will you*?' Another knowing look, and a touch of his nose with a finger. I ignored his fib about the Stringers, pretended to understand, shook my head and touched my nose. Grown-up stuff.

And that's why, while Mam and Dad were stripped down to the whatsits sunburning themselves on a Jetsun Super Summer Saver, we were trudging up that rotten concrete hill. It wouldn't have bothered me if the sun had never shone again.

'And why did it have to be the Stringers, Billy?' Mary said. 'Our Aunt Joyce, and *Smelly Lilly*.'

I shrugged my shoulders, kept walking.

Aunt Joyce had wanted to meet us off the

bus. But we're not little kids. We'd be getting enough of her once we were there without prolonging the agony. Seven days of solid boredom. Keeping clean, being tidy, and eating food just because it's good for you. One hundred and sixty-eight hours of do's and don'ts. Or rather don'ts and don'ts. Aunt Joyce had rules. Lots of rules. And they all began with don't. Don't put that there, don't make those noises, don't come in here with those feet. Don't even breathe, and if you die in the attempt don't do it on my best carpet. There was a rumour she had been married once. The bloke had done a bunk. I could believe that.

And if you think our Aunt Joyce sounds bad, our Aunt Lilly is worse. But hang on, I'm saving her up for later.

'Billy, if you don't wait for me I'm telling on you,' Mary said. How many times had I heard that one?

Mary trailed after me. She had Mog's cardboard box stuck under one arm, and she was dragging her suitcase behind her like it had an infectious disease. Well, it had been her idea to bring the cat – she could carry it. I should

have slowed down a bit and let her catch up. I
didn't.

'Oh, come on, Mary!' I shouted. 'We're
nearly there. Past the Union Hall,' Dad said.
'Third street on the left. Number twenty-eight
Orchard Views. It's a cinch!' I just hadn't
reckoned on the third street on the left being
so close to the top of the hill. My fingers
stopped working, and the skin on my hands
turned a nasty sort of purpley-green colour
where my suitcase's plastic handle had dug
permanent grooves. Stung like anything.

'Billy Tibbet, YOU JUST WAIT FOR ME!'
Mary was fit to burst. 'BILLY TIB . . .' She
suddenly stopped, swallowed the rest of her
sentence without chewing. We had turned the
corner into Orchard Views. Just ahead of us, a
tall skinny woman was in her front garden. She
was standing among a thin patch of flowers
that looked as if it had been laid out with a ruler
and a set square. She was waiting for us. Mary
forgot to shout. I forgot the sting in my hands.
Forgot everything. The world had shrunk, and
all that was left was that tall skinny woman.
Mzzzz Joyce Stringer . . . our Aunt Joyce.

'William, Mary . . . Yoo hoo.' Her voice sliced the air like a rusty knife. Huh, this was it then. I took a long deep breath – my last taste of freedom – and pushed Mary forward. 'Come along, children . . . wipe your feet, shoes off, slippers on, suitcases straight upstairs . . . Have yourselves a nice wash. And don't leave that *there*, dear.'

Mog was tipped out of her box and into the back yard like a bag of old scraps. 'For the duration,' Aunt Joyce said. Then she added, 'Oh, and when you're done, pop into the dining room and say hello to your Aunt Lilly.'

Lucky cat.

'Hello, Aunt Lilly,' I said.

'Hello, Aunt Lilly,' Mary said.

We just stood, still as we could, and looked. We never moved much when we visited the Stringers. The whole house was . . . well, it was *clean* and sort of untouchable. It felt as if no matter where you were, or what you were doing, you were messing things up.

The effect wasn't helped by the stink. THORNTON AND TURNBULL'S UNIVERSAL

SPIRIT. A *single squirt gets rid of ALL the dirt*. Its stench was everywhere. Reminded me of the dissected rats in the biology lab at school. Aunt Joyce swore by it.

The Stringers' dining room was no different to the rest of the house. It was neat and tidy, with matching sets of everything laid out on the table, ready for dinner.

'Is she awake, Billy?' Mary asked. 'Say something else to her.'

'I can't think of anything else,' I said.

Smelly Lilly was sitting at the far end of the room. Aunt Lilly. If she really was our aunt. I always thought Mam and Dad got a bit lost when it came to our Aunt Lilly. Something twice removed from a cousin's uncle on your Mam's side, Dad had said. Mam said she wasn't. Lived abroad for years, married that lad of your Walter's, Dad had said. Mam said she hadn't. Anyway, Aunt Lilly's a hundred and fifty years old at least, I reckon. Dead bodies have got more life in them. Her face was all buckled up and crumpled. Only her hands ever moved, and they never stopped, endlessly picking and fiddling like they were feeling for something

7

she had lost. And there was a thick mouldy sort of smell hanging around her, a smell that even Universal Spirit couldn't budge. She never spoke. She just sat there, stuck to her grotty old armchair. Right in the corner where the sun never gets, her black, hollowed-out eyes staring at nothing. Gave us the willies.

'Coming through, coming through!' Aunt Joyce's voice suddenly burst into the room on its own. The rest of her was only halfway out of the kitchen, weighed down by a big panful of something very heavy. 'Now, we are all going to try my special Grain Pulse and Soya Bean Pot, *aren't we*?'

– TWO –
Cuckoo Clocks and Picked Up Socks

I suppose you can get used to anything. Even Aunt Lilly, if you just ignore her. We got through dinner all right. And tea. And supper. Aunt Joyce even let us watch telly for half an hour, before sending us to bed.

Only now, I couldn't sleep. It was three o'clock. Exactly three o'clock. The absolute dead of the night. How did I know? A cuckoo clock in the Stringers' front room called out the time every hour, every half hour and every quarter hour. Its weak wooden *cu-coo* came up the stairs, through the walls of my bedroom, and dripped, plop, right into my ears. And on top of that, the house never stopped creaking – old floorboards and that. It sounded like somebody was forever creeping about on the landing, listening at your door. Well, I'd decided, tomorrow that cuckoo was going to die a painful death.

I wondered if Mary was still awake. But I didn't go to look. That was another *don't*. Don't leave your room in the middle of the night. 'Your Aunt Lilly wouldn't like it,' Aunt Joyce had said. Daft. What about the bog? I couldn't see our Mary holding out all night without the bog.

Cu-coo, *cu-coo*. Quarter past three.

The sheets on my bed were starched rigid and rubbed like cardboard. And somehow the clothes I'd taken off had been picked up off the floor, neatly folded, and put away in drawers.

I worked my way out of the sheets, sat up on the bed, and pulled open the window. The moon was shining. It needn't have bothered. Orchard Views at night was the same as Orchard Views by day, only the muddy red-bricks had turned to muddy grey-bricks. And as for the orchard view? Huh! There was no orchard. There wasn't even a tree. Not one! And there was *no* view. Just two rows of terraced houses staring at each other across the street. All exactly the same too. All that is, except for one . . . the house opposite. Odd that. In the dark that house was darker than all the rest. And it was the only one with a garden wall. A wall so high you couldn't see in at the downstairs windows. Not that I wanted to. Nobody had lived there for years.

At teatime Aunt Joyce had told us about their neighbours, and how we weren't to go playing round their doors giving them trouble. This side of the street was the even numbers, that side the odds. Directly opposite was number twenty-seven. The house had belonged to a strange old woman called Jenny Haniver. Until that is, one day, she just wasn't there any more. Aunt Joyce had been a bit vague on that point. The old woman had probably died, like old people do, and the house had been empty ever since. 'That house is a blight on the whole street,' she had said. 'It's a disgrace, a carbuncle, a festering rat trap.' She had grabbed a bottle of Thornton and Turnbull's Universal Spirit, and fingered it like a lethal weapon.

Cu-coo, cu-coo. Half past three.

I sat at that open window for a very long time. Nothing happened. Nothing was ever going to happen. Not at the Stringers'.

11

Cu-coo, cu-coo.

Much later . . . still nothing happened.

Cu-coo, cu-coo.

But then . . . something did.

Somewhere a hinge chittered, squeaked for just an instant. A gate, no one was meant to hear, inched open in the darkness. I sat bolt upright, suddenly alert. It was a daft idea, but I was sure the sound had come from the direction of the empty house.

Something was moving. Something or somebody. Feeling its way very, very slowly, following the heavy black shadow of the garden wall. I couldn't see it, but it was there all right.

Halfway up the street a black-and-white cat strolled out into the light of a street lamp. Huh, it was only our Mog. Then, in the next blink, she was gone. Not moved. *Disappeared.* Not strolled away. *Vanished.* One moment she was there, the next she wasn't. I shuddered, head to toe, like I'd been stroked by an icy black finger. Then the light of the street lamp went out.

I felt myself swaying. I threw my head back

12

and gulped down a breath of the cold night air. As I did, I found myself staring, way up into the sky – at least the moon was still in the place I expected it to be.

Snap!

And then it wasn't. Just a dirty great big gaping black hole.

I must have flaked out. I don't remember any more . . .

THREE

Jenny Haniver

'Oh yes! And I suppose the cow jumped over it . . . and then the dish ran away with the spoon.' Mary laughed, banging her mug against her cereal bowl and waving them about under my nose like a little baby.

'Don't play with the breakfast dishes, *dear*. You'll only upset your Aunt Lilly.' Aunt Joyce's voice worked itself between the kitchen and the dining room on wires.

Mary hadn't believed a word I'd said. And worse, she was playing silly beggars. I wanted to stick her head down the bog and flush it.

'All right then,' I said. 'If I'm making it all up where's our Mog?'

'Oh, she's always getting lost.' Mary was laughing again. 'Or maybe she's hiding under the table with the moon. Or behind Aunt Lilly's chair . . . no, there's no moon down there.'

I wasn't going to play her silly game. 'I knew I shouldn't have bothered telling a stupid girl,'

I said, scowl turning to daggers. She threw the daggers right back.

I had decided to keep it to myself, forget all about it. In the daylight there was nothing special about number twenty-seven. Its high garden wall put the empty house in shadow even in the blazing sunshine. The whole house was in such a rotten state, it was probably going to drop to bits at any second. *And* the hinges of the garden gate were thick with rust. But so what? It had been abandoned for years. That was how it should look. And as for disappearing moons and Mog and stuff? Well, that was just daft.

The trouble was, those icy black fingers had rested on my shoulder and they wouldn't let go.

So, I had told Mary everything.

Aunt Joyce launched herself into the room carrying a whopping-great sack of home-made muesli. It looked like dried-up rabbit droppings, tasted like cardboard. I ate it anyway. Funny really, yesterday the Stringers had been number one on my list of *worsts*. Ahead of the hole in the ozone layer, the daft presenters on children's telly and Dad's sweaty socks. But now, after last night, they were . . . normal. Aunt Joyce in her blue cotton overall and bright red rubber gloves. And Aunt Lilly, all fingers, picking and fiddling, stuck in her old armchair. Just the daft Stringers, with their Thornton and Turnbull's Universal Spirit, and their book of rules.

Mary was going to believe me. She was. Whether she wanted to or not . . .

'I can't see anything,' Mary said. 'And you're breaking my arm.'

'You're just not looking.' I twisted her arm up her back until the tears came, and frog-marched her out of the Stringers' front garden and up the street. How else was I going to get Mary to listen to me?

'*There*,' I said, pointing to the hole in the pavement where the lamppost had stood.

'There what? There's nothing *there*,' she said. 'Just a stupid hole.'

'Exactly – a hole.' Voices were getting louder.

'I think there's a hole in your head. Now let me go or I'm telling.'

'Look, Mary! It's the hole left when the lamppost disappeared – just after Mog.' I stopped. Cold as stone. Was it just me? All in my head? Loony-bin Billy? No! Mary had to believe me. She had to.

'Right – I'll prove it,' I said. The fact that I couldn't wasn't going to stop me.

'You're a pig, Billy,' Mary squealed. She swung back her leg and kicked in with her heel.

'Ow!' That stopped me. Suddenly we were a mass of flailing arms and legs. All nips and kicks, tugs and pushes. We keeled over, crashed straight through a rust-stained wooden gate. As we fell the gate swung shut, and the sun was gone. Quicker than clicking an on switch to off.

We were behind the garden wall of number twenty-seven.

'Mary – you OK?' I was whispering now.
'Pig.'
'Mary?'
'Cut my leg.'
'Sorry.'
'Pig.'

I seemed to have landed on the lid of an iron dustbin. I could taste the sourness of its rusted metal. Slowly the solid blackness turned into lumps of dirty, colourless grey. The garden was made up of bits of old rubbish and broken concrete. Then the face of the house loomed up, as friendly as a gravestone. One of the large downstairs windows was broken, the rest were just dull, lifeless, thick with years of dirt. There were only the ghosts of rooms behind them now.

Mary was leaning against the wall of the house, holding her leg with one hand while trying to poke her nose in at the broken window. If there was one thing she liked better than an argument, it was a neb-about in somebody else's business.

'Ouch,' she yelped, jumping backwards. 'That flippin' prickly stuff stuck right in me.' The skeleton of a climbing rose still clung to the brick work. It was a long time dead.

'SSSHHHHHH,' I said. 'Don't make so much noise. Someone'll hear us.'

'Shush yourself. There's been nobody in here for yonks ... Give me a bunk up to this

18

window, Billy. I can't see a thing from down here.'

I never got the chance. There was a shout . . . and another . . . and then another. We froze, rooted where we stood. But the shouting wasn't aimed at us. It was muffled, distant, inside the house. *Inside the empty house*.

'You . . . you don't think it's *her*, do you, Billy?' Mary whispered, hardly finding her voice. 'That Jenny Haniver come back?' I didn't answer.

Up on tiptoes I peered in through the broken window. The room was bare. That didn't surprise me. Bare, not empty.

'Open up. Blast you – OPEN UP.' The voice roared, and behind it breath rasped and crackled like dry sticks. Someone was standing there, back turned towards us, almost hidden in the gloom. It might have been a woman, but not much of a one. More a bundle, a rag-bag of bits, a sort of walking jumble sale.

'I'm warning you . . .' The breath sucked and blew dangerously. 'How many lifetimes have I lurked among the darkest shadows of this putrid world? How many, made do with petty mischief? Bored myself with silly pranks and simple trickery. Played a devil's peek-a-boo! What fun is there in that?' The crackle of breath became a bubbling, snotty-nosed sniff. 'Aaah! But then you crept into this world. Slipped quietly in, and thought it safe to lose yourself in hiding. Well . . . you could not hide from me. *Could you?* I searched you out. I found you. And now, now there are new games for me to play. So – FLAMIN'-WELL-OPEN!'

'What's she going on about, Billy?' Mary hissed at me through clenched teeth. 'Sounds like a right divvy. And who's she yelling at?'

'How on earth should I know!' I hissed back. 'I can't see anybody. If you'd just shut up for a minute though, and listen, we might find out.'

Jenny Haniver – if it really was Jenny Haniver – began to stomp noisily up and down. She became a mad woman and bounced across the room: jumping, kicking, twirling, spinning. Her hands yanking at something clasped between them. Whipped-up dust rolled and crashed through the air in miniature thunderstorms. She went on and on, banging, crashing about. Screeching at the top of her voice. Until, finally, her breath became so desperate she was forced to slither to a stop. Whatever it was all about – it hadn't worked.

She was close to the window now. I could see what was in her hands. A book. A small, leather-bound book.

'Please, just another little word . . . or a tiny little picture . . . I promise to be good this time,' she said, very, very softly, as if she was coaxing a baby out of its chocolate. Didn't make much sense to me. Her hands tugged. The book didn't open. Her hands tugged again. The book didn't . . . no, the book *wouldn't* open. Not your everyday ordinary sort of a book.

Then she was screeching again. 'Do as I command you! I stole you from a fool! A fool who does not know what you are. But I do. I DO. And you WILL open.'

The book stayed firmly shut.

'*Bah!*' The word was poison. 'Useless, stubborn—' She flung the book into the air and for a split second it seemed to hang there, nailed to the spot. Pierced by the stare of a single blood-red eye – just a slit in her crooked

21

face. Those icy black fingers ran up and down my back again. That look might have been murder. The split second lasted forever.

What happened next is still a bit of a blur. I reckon something told me to do it. Something I still don't really understand. I reached in through the broken window and snatched the book out of the air.

'Run for it Mary,' I shrieked. We ran all right. Ran, neck and neck, feet thumping concrete. Something close behind us. Ran, crashing heavily through the gate. The sting of sunlight. The crackle of that voice. The one word spoken. Then Mary gone. Not a hair, not a button, not the cut on her leg. Just gone.

Then standing in the front room with the Stringers without knowing how I got there. Blurting out the whole miserable tale. Aunt Lilly's empty black eyes stared right through me. But a smile spread across Aunt Joyce's face like dry bread curling at the edges. A dishonest grown-up smile – pretending to believe.

'But it's true, I tell you,' I tried to pull the book out of my pocket. Sure proof. I got no further. Aunt Joyce suddenly towered over me.

The smile was gone. Her face was a very dangerous-looking shade of purple.

'Billy – are those outdoor shoes?' The news that her niece had disappeared into thin air, and was lost and gone forever, had passed through her like water down a drainpipe. What she could see with her own eyes – clumps of muck on her best carpet – had not.

And then *her* face was at the window. Jenny Haniver.

Somehow, I reached the back door, was across the yard, and out into the back lane. I charged down the street. Crossed roads I knew, and then roads I didn't. Feet pounding. Head pounding. Things flashing in front of me as if they were real . . . Aunt Joyce's dry bread smile . . . that staring red eye . . . the crack of dry sticks . . . and Mary.

'MARY,' I yelled.

My head was so full up I thought it would burst. Red hot tears scalded my cheeks as they ran down my face. What the heck was I going to do now? My legs were running, it seemed so simple just to let them keep on going . . .

FWOMP!

– FOUR –

Zonked!

'Well what's this then? – squirms like an eel.'

'Should watch where it's going, barging about all over the place.'

'Looks like a cry-baby to me.'

'Or a fish.'

'Or a water rat with a soggy face.'

'Keep a tight hold of it.'

'Aye, or stick nettles down its back.'

When I came to myself I was lying on the ground surrounded by a forest of skinny pink legs. I had heard the voices. Girls' voices. I was sure of that.

'I'll shove nettles down the back of your knickers and see how you like that,' I said. I was in the mood to clout somebody. I– didn't.

'Not a very friendly water rat, is he?'

'Needs a lesson, that one.'

'Aye, or–'

'Let him up!' a new voice demanded. The forest of legs shuffled apart. Behind them stood

24

a small girl. Very small, and very round, almost a ball. On her face was a pair of swotty-looking wire-rimmed specs with thick milk-bottle lenses. 'Let him up, *I said.*' Her voice was as thin as paper, and she looked down at the ground as she spoke. She was more embarrassed by the tears on my face than I was. I scrambled to my feet.

I had run down a letch – a back lane – with a high red-brick wall running along one side of a tarmac path, and the broken wooden fence of an allotment on the other. And then there was this odd bunch. Four of them, and all girls. The sort you can nick-name as easy as look at them. There was Swot of course, the one with the specs. Then the one who had started all the cheek – Lippy Jane, I called her. Then Conk, a scrap of a lass with the beaut' of a cracked scab right on the end of her nose. And lastly Sprog, a young'un, nothing more than a bairn. It wasn't much of a gang, more like something the morning tide had washed up.

'You're not from round here,' Swot said. It might have been a question, and I could have bluffed it, or done another runner, but, well –

what choice was there? I needed help and they were all I had.

I told them about dark empty houses . . . about disappearing cats and missing lamp-posts . . . about creepy figures, stolen books . . . and about Mary. By the time I had finished they were all gaping like goldfish. Eyes as big as plates stuck out on stalks. And if I somehow forgot to mention the moon, well, maybe you can have too much of a good thing.

'The whole lamppost, eh? – zonked, just like that.'

'A load of old codswallop, you mean.'

'Who's going to make up something like that?'

'He's a ruddy nutter. Should get the poliss.'

'Aye, or find those nettles.'

'Eee, the poor cat though.'

'I'll bet he hasn't even *got* a sister.'

Swot stood quietly by herself, waiting for the others to blow themselves out. When they had, she looked down at the ground and said simply, 'Prove it.' I was beginning to see why she was their leader. It was make or break time.

I dipped my hand into my pocket and pulled

out the leather-bound book. There was dead quiet, as if the whole world had stopped breathing. We were all staring. It was just like the tatty old books you find on the shelves marked *Reference Only* in the local library. The kind of books that are so old they drop to bits before you even touch them. The kind the toffee-nosed library assistants chase you away from, just in case.

There was no title on the cover. No words, anyway. Just a funny jumble of symbols. Stars, triangles, moon shapes and stuff. Didn't mean anything much to me – half-rubbed away with age.

'I wonder what's in it?' said Conk, in such a quiet voice you'd have thought she was in church. I tried to turn the pages to look inside. They wouldn't budge, stuck fast. I'd been a slow starter, but I was beginning to catch on. I remembered Jenny Haniver behind the broken window at number twenty-seven. She'd nearly burst a blood vessel trying to shift its pages. This book had a mind of its own. And right now it didn't want to open up, so it wasn't going to.

'Probably magic or something,' Sprog whispered hopefully.

'Magic nothing,' sniggered Lippy Jane. 'It's just a stupid old book with all its pages glued together – he probably did it himself.'

'You have a go then – you open it,' I said, thrusting the book into her hand. She didn't even try. Instead, she deliberately dropped it, kicked it hard and sent it skittering along the path.

'See,' she said, still sniggering. 'Just a book with its pages all stuck up.'

Before I could move Sprog went scrambling after it. Hurriedly, she picked it up, rubbing the dirt off onto her dress. 'It's all right. It's not bust.' I could have given Lippy Jane a right mouthful then. I nearly did. But you see, as Sprog cleaned the book up, it fell open in her hands. Fell open, as easy as that. All the sniggers were gone.

For a moment Sprog stared eagerly into it, but eagerness faded. 'It *is* some kind of a library book,' she said, her face leaking disappointment. 'Somebody's written in it, in big creaky letters. PLEASE RETURN THIS

BOOK AND HELP SAVE.'

'Help save?' said Conk. 'Help save what?'

'Help save *nothing*. Just help save,' said Sprog.

'Give it here! There must be something else.' I snatched the book back off her, and read the words over and over again. As if on the twentieth time they might suddenly decide to say something different. 'Please return this book and help save. Help save . . . *Help save.*' They didn't.

Conk and Lippy Jane swapped awkward glances, like I really was a nutter.

'I think . . .' said Swot, scratching the back of her legs, thoughtfully. 'I think, if you want to know what the help save bit is, you've got to do the please return bit first.'

'What?'

'Please return this book,' she said. 'That's what it says, so that's what you've got to do. Return the book to whoever it really belongs to.'

'But I don't know who it really belongs to,' I said. 'Jenny Haniver stole the flippin' thing. I don't even know where to start looking.'

'It's like a quest. Or an adventure,' said Sprog.

'More like a ruddy nightmare, if it's a rotten old library book,' said Lippy Jane.

'It's still a good game, though,' said Sprog. I tried to smile as if I really meant it. It wasn't a silly game, but a game was better than nothing.

Swot started scratching the back of her legs again.

Twenty minutes later we turned the corner into Orchard Views. The lasses were in such a tizzy of excitement they were fizzing like pop.

Swot had come up with a plan. It was dead simple too. We were, er . . . going to lie, going to tell the Stringers the gang had seen everything from the very start. *Corroborated Evidence*. That's what we needed. Aunt Joyce would have to believe me then, and do – do whatever grown ups should do when things like sisters are disappeared into nothingness. We'd probably all be on the telly. They'd make a photofit out of Jenny Haniver. Then the real owner of the book would come forward and solve the whole mystery. We'd get Mary back.

And there might even be a reward.

Orchard Views was looking very, very ordinary. In the sun the windows of the houses winked at us as we passed. A bunch of women were gabbling at a garden gate. And I could hear the bloke at number forty mucking about in his bathroom. Huh, nothing terrible could possibly have happened in this street.

'Look, look,' Sprog shrieked, 'there's the hole in the ground where the lamppost stood. It *is* true.'

'Council probably dug it up,' said Lippy Jane.

'What about that, then?' Conk was pointing. 'That must be *her* house. A dark shadow lay across the face of number twenty-seven like an ugly black scar.

'That house gives me the willies.'

'Aunt Joyce,' I called out. I had to do something, before their fizz went flat and I found myself on my own again. 'Aunt Joyce – are you there?' Her thin regiment of flowers still guarded number twenty-eight, same as ever. I grabbed the shining front door knocker. The door fell away under my touch.

It was open.

The Stringers' front door was never *ever* left open. That was a rule. Horrible uneasy feelings crept into my stomach. The sort of feelings that tell you things are getting out of hand and there is nobody there to help. The sort of feelings that tell you the worst is still to come.

Swot was standing next to me. The rest of the gang were frantically scrabbling into a single file behind her.

Together we stepped through the open doorway.

'Auntie?'

The hallway was empty. Completely empty. No carpets. No coat stand. No neat little telephone. No Thornton and Turnbull's Universal Spirit. Nothing. The front room was the same. And the living room. In fact the whole house felt empty. Empty of everything. Including the Stringers.

We worked our way slowly along the hallway towards the last door. The kitchen door. Against the bare floorboards every step we took made an awkward brittle thud. Outside the sun was burning hot, but inside, in that hallway, it was suddenly very cold.

'I want to go home,' Conk whispered, picking nervously at her scab.

'I never wanted to come in the first place,' said Lippy Jane. Given half a chance I think they would all have legged it. I didn't give them half a chance.

I pulled open the kitchen door.

Sprog leapt backwards in such a state of fright she nearly left her pants behind her.

Standing in the open doorway was Jenny Haniver. Her single slit of an eye, now grown huge and swollen, took us all in with one look. Her dry-stick breath snapped and crackled, as she swallowed great mouthfuls of air in her excitement. I wanted to move. To turn away. To run. But I couldn't. I waited. I waited . . .

And then the dried-up old face moved. Not much. A muscle, not used to the effort, twitched and her thin lipless mouth opened. It was a smile. Crocodiles smile like that just before they twist your head off.

'Hello, Billy. So . . . you've brought home your Auntie's book at last,' she lied.

'An-An-Auntie?' The word didn't want to come out of my mouth. 'You're – you're not

33

my aunt. And it's not your book.'

The red eye narrowed, and her smile flicked off and then on again, as if she was thinking. I gripped the little book as tightly as I could, sure that that was the only reason something really, really horrible hadn't just happened to us.

'You been telling your tales again, Billy?' Jenny Haniver croaked, taking half a step towards the lasses. 'Of course I'm his aunt. Who else would I be?' Her smile widened with her lie.

'Oh yes, and I suppose Mary's just a tale as well, is she?' Swot blurted.

Jenny Haniver sucked in another rattling breath. 'There was an accident. A car. Hit a lamppost . . . *poor* Mary. *Poor* Mog too.' She moved another half-step closer. 'Never got over it, did you, Billy?'

Swot, Lippy Jane, Conk and Sprog – they were looking at me now. Questioning. Not sure. They began backing away towards the front door. This was all too horrible, and worse. Much, much worse.

'It's all lies,' I cried out. 'Lies, *lies*, LIES!'

Jenny Haniver saw her chance and threw

herself at me. As she lunged an odd thing happened – it was as if a mask she'd been wearing had suddenly slipped. She really did only have one huge eye. She wasn't hunched up and twisted, making her *look* as if her eye was in the middle of her face. Her eye *was* in the middle of her face. A face with no nose, two sunken black dots for nostrils, and more wrinkles than a pan full of spaghetti. Her gnarled hands closed around mine, crushing them in a grip bigger than my dad's. Then she tugged. I flew through the air, still clinging desperately to the book. I didn't let go. I couldn't, not if I wanted to see Mary or the Stringers ever again.

'Maybe you don't really want your sister back?' Jenny Haniver growled, not bothering with another lie. She tugged again. I couldn't hold on to the book much longer.

'Come on!' Swot yelled.

The lasses jumped, all at once, grabbing for my ankles, my trousers, my shirt sleeves, anything they could get a hold of. Between them I became a human tug-of-war. As Jenny Haniver heaved one way, the lasses heaved the other. She pulled again. They pulled again.

'Bah! I'll, I'll, I'll . . .' Jenny Haniver screeched, her red eye jumping and popping angrily inside her head. The lasses gave one last, desperate tug.

And then it happened.

'—!'

In her anger, Jenny Haniver spat out a different kind of word. Just one. The same awful word she had rasped at Mary. A word far too dangerous ever to be written down.

The last thing I remember was the rasp and rake of her breath, and her smile curdling. Then nothing.

FIVE

Where Mary Went

'Mary . . . MARY . . .' I couldn't shout any louder. 'WHERE ARE YOU?' I was sure I was supposed to be looking for her. It had suddenly become dark. Why is it always horribly dark when rotten things happen? I'd been in my aunt's house – hadn't I? There had been a terrible struggle and . . . and . . . Slowly I began to remember. Swot . . . and the rest of the gang . . . and that Jenny Haniver with her scuffed sandpaper voice.

Deathly quiet now. And alone.

'This'll teach Mam and Dad a lesson – they'll think twice about going off without me again,' I shouted into the silence. 'I'm not scared. I'm not going to cry.' My voice didn't travel very far. The darkness swallowed up the words the way fat lads wolf down chocolate. And I was scared.

It was odd, I was sure I was moving. At least my arms and legs were going through the motions. But where was the slop clop sound of my feet hitting the ground? The answer was easy. There wasn't any ground. 'Oh, ruddy heck . . .' There wasn't any ground, and there wasn't any sky. No up. No down. I was running right through the middle of nowhere. I felt sick.

A good old blubber was beginning to seem like a pretty good idea, when the tiniest of orange specks caught my eye. A pinprick of light in all that darkness. And getting larger. Larger, and closer. It became more than a pinprick. Long and skinny with a big dollop of orange stuck at one end. It was a lamppost. And beneath it, an outline under its orange glow, sat a cat. Not just any cat. Our Mog.

Just then the ground caught me up. I tripped, bounced, flipped right over and smacked into the lamppost, bum first. Worse than any mam's slap on a bare leg. My backside thought it had been paddled with a cricket bat, and my head was rolling. Sour sicky ooziness glooped and slopped about inside of me. I really was going to be sick.

Mog hadn't moved a whisker. There was a

funny, puzzled look about her, almost as if she was going to ask me a question. And then . . . she did.

'You don't happen to have a bite to eat on you?'

That's when I was sick.

Mog gave herself a quick embarrassed lick, and then, embarrassed at her own embarrassment, gave herself another.

'That a no then, Billy?' she asked.

I tried to give her one of Dad's cold hard stares. I was sick again. Mog stood up very slowly, threw her tail high into the air, and walked out of the lamplight and into the darkness.

'Oh please, don't go, I'm, I'm . . .' (I didn't know what I was – except very sick). For a moment Mog's voice drifted back out of the darkness.

'Are you sure you haven't got just a tiny nibble?'

'Of course I'm sure,' I said.

'Pity. Still, no harm in asking . . .' Her voice trailed away. She was gone.

'Good riddance to bad rubbish,' I said. I was

annoyed, frightened, sick and excited – all mixed in together. Well, I had just fallen out of the sky, and cats can't talk can they? I managed to get to my feet without being sick again – that was something.

'Anyway, I like being on my own,' I said to myself. Didn't sound very convincing.

I stood and watched the lamp, its sad little light could only tickle the darkness . . . How had I not seen it before? More obvious than the scab at the end of Conk's nose. The cat. The lamppost. She was *my* cat and so this was *my* lamppost. Last night I really had seen them disappear, and now they were here. And . . . and I was here too. Wherever here was. I tried to look beyond the lamplight, out into the darkness. If the lamppost was here, and Mog was here, then maybe the moon was here too and . . . Well, I looked. There was no moon.

'No moon. No Aunt Lilly. No Aunt Joyce . . . And no Mary.'

How long was I alone under that lamppost? I don't know. Yonks and yonks. Long enough to stop feeling sick, to feel an icy coldness tip-toeing around inside of me. Not an outside weather-cold creeping in, no, an inside sort of coldness creeping out.

And then, suddenly, Mog bounced back into the light. She was in such a state of excitement she couldn't stand still.

'Miamff mmiamff mmmfff.' There was something sticking out of her mouth. 'Mmiamff mmmfff mmmfff mmiammfff.' Well, I know Mog, and the kind of stuff she fetches home. Dead blackbirds without heads. Or live sparrows, with their wings so badly chewed they can only hobble about the kitchen floor like broken clockwork toys.

'You rotten cat – you let that go!'

'Mmiammfff mmff mmfff.' She bounced out of the light, then back in again, before finally dropping her package. 'Look! – Look what I've got.' If a cat can grin, she grinned then, from ear to ear.

Between her paws was a very old, very tatty, and only slightly chewed, leather-bound book. *The* book.

'I suppose it is yours, is it?' Mog asked, rather hoping that it wasn't.

'Mine?' Had I really brought it with me?

41

Dropped it when I hit the ground?

'Mur-dle . . . Clay's . . . Lit-tle . . . Book . . .' Mog began slowly, as if she was reading.

'And I suppose that's on the cover, is it?' I laughed. I could remember looking at the cover, with its symbols, signs and that. There were no words.

'As a matter of fact, yes . . . yes, it is,' she said, indignantly.

'Oh ha ha,' I said. 'Not just a talking cat, but a cat that can read now eh?'

'Shows what you know.' Mog was getting annoyed. 'Self-taught I am. Been reading for ages. Mind you, I would have got on a whole lot quicker if certain people hadn't kept pushing me off their newspapers every time I sat down. Titles is *kid's* stuff – nothing to it.'

'All right then,' I said, 'what else does it say?'

'It says, Murdle Clay's Little Book . . . of . . . In-cre-di-bly . . . Use-ful . . . Words . . . and Pictures. And . . .' Mog smiled a very self satisfied smile, 'if you don't believe me you can look for yourself.'

I did. I picked the book up. Its pages were stuck tight shut, just as I expected them to be.

But on the front cover, right at the top where before there had been nothing, were the spidery scratches of an old-fashioned ink pen. Handwriting. *Murdle Clay's Little Book of Incredibly Useful Words and Pictures*. That writing could have been a thousand years old.

'Who's Murdle Clay then?' Mog asked, still smiling at how clever she had been.

I couldn't answer, I didn't have one. I just mumbled, and turned the book over between my fingers. 'Oh yes, incredibly useful – a book with no way in!'

And then the book fell open. As easily as it had done for Sprog. Its pages flicked carefully over, as if it was looking for something. And when it got there it stopped.

The open page was – a mess. A slash and scrape of the same ancient handwriting on the cover. A scribbler's notes, without a top or bottom, start or finish. The writer must have gone at it from all sides at the same time. And in one heck of a hurry. Wherever the pen had been once in one direction it had been there again from the opposite direction. I think it was supposed to be a map, but it was a really rotten

43

attempt at a map. Long curling loops and scratches might have been the outlines of islands. There might have been a dotted line – a route to follow – complete with written directions. Named land marks. Standing stones. There might have been a forest. A river. Mountains and a moon. A tree with someone hiding in it. There might have been a Mog. An Aunt Joyce and an Aunt Lilly. Even a Billy Tibbet – there might even have been a Billy Tibbet standing under a lamppost. But that would have been daft, wouldn't it? *Wouldn't it?*

I remembered Swot scratching the back of her leg, working out that the book had to go back to its real owner; telling me to do the PLEASE RETURN bit, before I worried about the HELP SAVE. I'll tell you something, I didn't understand any of it. But I was sure that was it. That was what I had to do – return the book to its owner, return the book to Murdle Clay. And somehow, the book itself was showing me how to find him.

I should have looked at that page more carefully, taken more in, but I was never much good at that geography stuff and anyway scratched across the whole rotten mess, in blood-red letters, one word was screaming at me, desperate to be read. DANGER. Danger double-underlined. If it was meant to help, to make me feel better, it didn't work. The more I tried to make sense of it all, the more muddled up it got, until I wasn't sure I was looking inside the pages of a book at all.

Suddenly, all around me, the darkness was gone. And slap bang in the middle of the sky was the moon. Its face was pale and anxious, and puffed out, like it was trying really hard to blow light across the whole world.

The book snapped shut and wouldn't open up again. I stuffed it inside my shirt.

Now I could see that the lamppost was standing on the top of a mountain. A mountain among a world of mountains that tumbled away around it for ever. In fact mountains were about all I could see. Great tall things in all sorts of colours. Not proper mountain colours, but bright reds, yellows and oranges, and one – the biggest of them all – was Smartie-blue. When I looked at them properly they seemed to be standing deliberately apart, like a group of huffy giants not speaking to each other. And lying inbetween them all, wherever the mountains let the moonlight in, was a growing mask of fog. Now at their feet, now at their ankles, now higher still, creeping upwards as far as it dared go, smothering everything it touched. The whole scene was odd, pretty like a dream, and exciting. But wrong somehow. Wrong, even if I couldn't explain why. A bit like the old-fashioned cards people send at Christmas: kind of sad, even when all the faces are smiling.

Well, I suppose the book was right about the moon, and the lamppost, and the Billy Tibbet. So somewhere, underneath all that lot, there might just be a Murdle Clay, and a Mary, maybe even the Stringers too. There might just.

SIX

Rumbles, Tumbles and The Stairs Up

'A person up a tree . . . er, standing stones . . . er, a track . . .' I'd told Mog all about Mary and Jenny Haniver, about PLEASE RETURN, and HELP SAVE, and now I was trying to tell her what I remembered about the map. It wasn't very much.

We'd been walking for ages and ages. Years, probably.

I had discovered the one good thing about being lost at the top of a mountain. There was only one direction to go looking in – *down*. But we hadn't really got anywhere. Everywhere we went, the fog followed. Everything the book had shown me the fog was going to hide, like a guilty secret. And it was full of dark smudgy shapes, twisting and turning just out of the corner of my eye.

'You should have shown me the inside of that book,' Mog said. 'I expect you've been walking us round in circles.'

'No I haven't,' I said. 'We're still moving downhill. And anyway, it's my book, and I'll . . .'

But Mog wasn't listening to me. A funny puzzled look was stuck to her face again, and her ears were twitching. She was listening to something else.

The noise came slowly at first. A painful rumbling, grumbling about deep under the ground. Building and gathering, gathering to a roar. Worst case of indigestion I've ever heard. Then it suddenly stopped, and everything was quiet again.

There was nothing to do but keep walking.

And the fog came too. Slowly, as we made our way downhill, the smudgy shapes it was hiding changed – from rocks into bushes, from bushes into trees. Brittle branches crackled and snapped apart as we brushed past. The plants were shrivelled, the trees were dead, the ground was bone dry. There was something else I should have noticed – there was no bright sparkly colour to this mountain. No. Just a horrible mouldy old grey, like it was really, really ill or something.

I saw Mog's ears twitching before I heard the noise again. The earth belched. The ground under our feet moved. I was standing up, and then I was on my backside.

'MiiaaaOOOOWWWWW,' Mog cried out like she'd been scalded and disappeared into the fog. I could hear rocks falling, breaking apart. Even the trees wouldn't keep still. Their bones rattled and shook, and somewhere far off the weakest trees clashed against each other as they fell. I just sat and shook along with the rest and waited to see what would happen next.

Next, the rumbling stopped, as if to take a breath, and then the ground opened up in front of me. Something started crawling out. A huge muscle-knotted arm appeared, with a heavy shovel-hand as big as a garden spade stuck on the end. Then a head on a neck so thick it came straight up out of its stocky body. The head had eyes, as tiny as blackcurrants and as dead as nail-heads. I suppose it was a sort of an old man, or . . . or a rock troll, the same as you get in daft fairy stories. Anyway, he sat down on the edge of the hole he'd just climbed out of, poked his nose into the air and sniffed. It must have told him something.

'Right then you lot, up you come,' he said.

'Are you sure it's safe, Grundiggar,' an anxious voice replied from deep inside the hole, adding oddly, 'you haven't fallen off the end?'

'No, of course I haven't fallen off the end,' said Grundiggar, with a guffaw of a laugh as deep as my dad's boots. 'Or else I wouldn't be talking to you now, would I Bruggle?'

'Can't be too careful, husband,' said Bruggle, stiffly. 'This mountain's not safe, not a push and shove away from dust and ashes.' With that a whole family of faces with dead nail-head eyes appeared cautiously over the edge of the hole. There was a second rock troll almost as big as Grundiggar – that was Bruggle – and two small 'uns who must have been kids. There wasn't a single hair between them. Their grey skin looked rough, hard and worn, and was covered in wrinkles.

'Oh, look!' The small'uns pulled themselves out of the hole and ran across to a newly-scattered pile of rocks. Something like a smile passed between them and . . . well, they picked up a rock each and ate it. They swallowed it in one, without chewing.

'Steady now, steady,' said Grundiggar, the echo of his laugh bouncing around inside the hole. 'Leave some for Bruggle and me.' Then they were all at it – tucking into rocks like it was their Christmas dinner. Their great shovel-hands scooped them off the ground and broke them apart, and their long rough tongues snuffled the bits off their fingers with obvious delight.

'Deee-licious!' said the smallest of the small'uns, flicking a handful of gravel at his sister.

'Don't play with your food, dear,' Bruggle scolded, in a voice that didn't really mean it, and Grundiggar guffawed again, splitting a boulder in two between his teeth.

At that very instant the ground creaked, and a whole chunk of mountain caved in behind them. Thick black clouds of dust soared into the air. The dinner party was suddenly over. I heard the small'uns yell out, and the beat of Grundiggar's heavy legs as he stomped about. But the dust and the fog got a bit mixed up then and I didn't see the rock trolls again.

'I've found her,' a breathless voice blurted out behind me, nearly killing me with fright. Huh, it was just our Mog. 'I've found her,' she said again, 'that book of yours was right.'

'What?'

'There *is* a person up a tree – and it's your Mary! She won't come down though, thinks she's dreaming.'

Mog led me through a tight group of trees that stood at the edges of a small clearing. Here the fog had broken into little stagnant pools and the moonlight leaked in through the branch tops. In the middle of the clearing a pair of giant stones, bigger than double-decker buses, loomed up at us.

Mog stopped. 'She's up there.' The two stones were standing guard over a skinny withered little tree that stood between them.

'Are you sure?' I said, looking up at its mop-head of dead branches. 'I can't see anything.' Mog gave me one of her looks and sat down to watch. I walked all the way round the tree. 'Mary?' Her name crept out as a whisper. 'Mary Tibbet?'

Nothing.

'MARY TIBBET.' I shouted this time. There was a slight rustle and crack of twigs, and one of the branches appeared to drop. Not a branch. A leg. A pink, girl's leg – with a scratch. (Actually, with lots of scratches). I would have known that leg anywhere. 'Mary – it's me. Billy.' Now that I knew it was her I could see her more clearly. Funny, that. She looked a bit crumpled up and tatty, and had a red blotchy face – been blubbing. Couldn't blame her, I suppose.

'Mary . . . are you listening? It's ME. Your brother – BILLY.'

'No thank you,' she said her voice quietly polite, like she had been offered a rotten plain biscuit at my nan's house on a Sunday. 'I'm waiting for the Air Sea Rescue helicopter.'

'Mary, stop talking rubbish – and get yourself down here. You're not asleep, and this is not a dream.'

'Not today thank you, me mam says there's too many E numbers in bottled fizzy pop.'

'MARY.' I'd give her pop. If she wasn't going to come down on her own I was just going to

53

have to bring her down. The trunk of her tree was so skinny, when I shook it I could get the top to flop about drunk. My first go only shook her up a bit, so I did it again. The branches swayed and cracked, and for a split second there was dead silence, before they gave way completely. Mary thudded to the ground. I suppose it wasn't really the best way to do it, but it did get her down.

'Billy Tibbet – *I hate you.*'

'Huh, well, don't thank me for saving your life then.'

'I could've broken my flippin' neck.'

'But you didn't,' I said.

'I could have been smashed to pieces.'

'But you weren't.'

'Killed . . . OR WORSE!'

'But . . .'

'I'll get you back for this, Billy. If it takes for ever and ever. Just you wait. Just . . .'

Suddenly the ground groaned and creaked again.

'I think,' put in Mog quickly, before we could start our slanging match again, 'I think we'd better get out of here.'

'Our Mog just spoke,' Mary started. There wasn't time to explain, even if I could.

With the creaking came the crack of tree roots, and the ground broke open in a wide grimaced yawn. The hole began to swallow, and the trees and the huge standing stones began to disappear.

Getting out of there was not a bad idea, but – and it was a big but – where to?

I grabbed hold of Mary and started running. Running again! I suppose I was getting used to it – and at least it always got me somewhere. If Murdle Clay's book really had shown me an island then there must be a sea and maybe a boat or a raft or something.

The noises the ground made got worse with every footstep. Something was very, very wrong deep down inside, and it wasn't going to be fixed by an indigestion tablet. A giant wave of earth rose up around us, broke open and fell away again.

'Keep going, Mary,' I yelled, giving her another pull in encouragement. She didn't. She stopped dead. So did I. So did Mog. So did the ground. This wasn't an island. There wasn't any sea, or boats. When somebody tells you the world is round, don't believe them until you've seen it for yourself. The land had just stopped, like a cliff's edge. If we had taken just one more step . . .

At last I could see what had been wrong with the view from the lamppost. Oh yes, there were other mountains all right. I could still see them, with their reds and blues and oranges. The thing was they weren't connected to the one we were standing on. Each mountain – like a castle in the air – stood on its own, in an empty space only given body by the fog. And there was no way between them.

The ground groaned pitifully. A dying man on his death bed.

'Billy, I'm scared,' Mary said. 'What are we going to do?'

'I . . .' I was scared too.

Just then something fell out of my shirt and landed on the ground. *Murdle Clay's Little Book of Incredibly Useful Words and Pictures.* The tight grip the book had been holding on itself slackened, and the pages scattered. There were four words hurriedly scrawled in the corner of a page. Just four words: STAIRS UP. STAIRS DOWN.

'What does that mean?' Mary asked. She'd taken the words right out of my mouth.

'Er . . .' The ground rippled under our feet and lumps of loose rock disappeared over the cliff edge.

'Er . . . stairs up, stairs down. A riddle? A ri . . . no, not a riddle. Look for some stairs, Mary.'

'There aren't any stairs,' she said.

'If the book says stairs – then there's stairs.'

Mog suddenly bounded forward and took a flying leap right off the edge of the cliff. My mouth fell open with a clunk. She didn't fall. She was standing, quite happily, in mid-air. She gave another little jump. She really could have been climbing a staircase, *if* there had been a staircase there.

Quickly I grabbed the book, lifted a leg, and tried to take a step up. I fell flat on my face.

'I *told* you there was nothing there,' Mary said.

'You have to believe they're here,' Mog said. 'Just because you can't see them with your eyes

57

doesn't mean they're not.'

Mary lifted a leg, leant forward, pushed down – and fell flat on her face.

'Oh, come on – you're not even trying,' Mog laughed.

'I'll show you who's not trying.' I closed my eyes tight shut and began to think about the staircase at home. 'There *is* a staircase . . . there *is* a staircase . . . there *is* . . .' I lifted a leg and leant forward. I could feel something under my foot. A step. And then another, and then another . . .

'Watch it,' Mog cried, 'you're going to stand on me.' When I opened my eyes I really was standing off the ground.

'Come on up, Mary,' I shouted down to her, 'it's a cinch!'

'I . . . I don't think I can.'

'Just do what I did.'

Mary half-shut her eyes and said feebly, 'There . . . there *is* a staircase.' She lifted a leg off the ground, waggled it about a bit and put it down again.

'WELL, I CAN'T FEEL ANYTHING,' she yelled.

'Oh, come on.' I leant down, grabbed her by the scruff of the neck, and pulled.

'Ow . . . ow, I'm up, Billy. I can feel the rotten stairs. I can feel them. So get your great mitts off me before I clobber you one.'

'Come on then,' Mog said. She bounded up through the air as if she'd been born to invisible stairs. Slowly we followed.

I only looked back once. The moonlight was dabbing at the top of the mountain. It couldn't put any colour into its deathly sick-grey face. But there was something more than that. Down at the bottom a commotion was going on. Just where we had found the STAIRS UP the fog was licking and spitting. And tiny grey shapes – tiny grey rock troll shapes – were jigging up and down. I turned away and tried not to think about it.

We plodded on, and up. Up and up for ever. Well, up and up until the back of my legs ached like mad. 'Do you want a rest, Mary?' I said.

'No I don't,' she said. I could tell by her voice that she was just being awkward. 'I want to know where we're going, I want to know how Mog can talk, I want to know about that book.

I want to know everything, Billy, and . . .'

So, I told her everything. Everything I knew that is. When I finished there was a very long thoughtful silence. Then at last Mary said, 'Can I carry that Murdle Thingummy's book for a bit? Seeing as I'm going to help you find him. Please Billy, can I?'

'If you want,' I said. I took the book out of my shirt and gave it to her. We were a team now. Well, at least, until the next scrap.

SEVEN

The Battle at the Boodies' Den

Nothing interesting happened for ages. We just kept on going up, and up, and up, forever.

Until I suddenly realised the stairs had become real. I mean, I could actually see them for real. They were made of stone, the steps worn away in great scoops as if a hundred million pairs of feet had walked on them. And there was a funny smell in the air. The damp, mouldy-old-stone smell of empty churches on freezing cold Sunday mornings. Mog was suddenly slinking behind me, her tail swishing in uneasy jerky fits.

'I think we've reached the top, Billy,' Mary whispered, and as she spoke something made her slip Murdle Clay's book into the pocket of her dress.

A thin slice of yellow light spread out in front of us, poking through the gap in a broken wooden door. I edged forward.

It wasn't proper light – not electric or

sunlight or anything – no, not even moonlight. It was old and rotten, if light can be old and rotten, not really coming from anywhere and only hanging about the doorway because there was nowhere else for it to go. The door itself was big and heavy, and hung cock-eyed from iron hinges on one side, and from a huge rust-frozen lock on the other. Its wood was as dry and brittle as a cream cracker, and had splintered clean down the middle. There was a sign stuck clumsily to it. It was hand-done, and so faded I could only just make it out. It read: NO CALLERS. THIS MEANS YOU. Huh, there hadn't been callers at that door for a hundred years.

I didn't really know what to do next, so I did the only thing I could think of. I knocked on the door. A deep rolling echo boomed out, resounding angrily again and again. And as the noise faded away it was replaced by an equally deep and very resentful silence. This door did not like being knocked on.

Mog began edging herself, bottom first, towards the top of the stairs. I stood on her tail. 'MiaaOOWW.' We were all in this together, and that was how it was going to stay.

We waited. Slowly, the silence behind the door began to change. A change so slight that at first I couldn't say what it was. A movement? A wind? A voice? I only knew that out of the silence a new sound was creeping. An uncertain shuffling sound, not used to being made. The shuffling stopped just behind the door. Someone was listening.

'Read the sign and . . . and sling your hook,' a voice barked. It was a small voice, but a small voice pretending to be a very big voice. Mary was good at doing that, and I didn't let *her* get away with it.

'No,' I said, 'we won't.' It was a few startled moments before the voice spoke again.

'Something said no,' it said.

'I did,' I said, 'me – Billy Tibbet.'

'It says it's a Billy Tibbet,' said a second voice.

'Don't want no Billy Tibbets round here – so hop it,' said the first voice. 'Skulking behind people's doors . . .'

'Aye,' said the second voice. 'We don't want no *lurkers* . . . thieves and murderers out to steal a person's rightful property – so shove off.'

'We're not lurkers,' said Mog. 'Or thieves, or murderers – I'm a cat, and he *is* a Billy Tibbet.'

'And there's me too – Mary Tibbet.'

'There's another one,' said the first voice, 'could be hundreds of them out there, *lurking* about.'

'There aren't hundreds of us – there are just three,' Mary snapped, 'and we're tired, and we're hungry . . . and we're just trying to find Murdle Clay to give him his stupid little book back!' That was a mistake. That was a very big mistake. Mary and her flamin' big gob. With a muffled shriek that sounded just like '*Bones and blood*,' the voices behind the door fell into a stiff shocked silence and stayed there for ages.

'What on earth did you tell them that for?' I said. I really could have thumped her this time.

'Well, that is why we're here isn't it? That, and to find the Stringers. And anyway, I am hungry, *and* tired *and* I need the bog!' Mary's got a great knack of making every word sound like blame.

Beyond the door there was a lot more silence, more shuffling, more whispering, and then . . . a decision was made.

'Tired are you? Hungry? Poor, *poor* Mary. Why don't you come in and *rest* yourself, put your feet up . . .' This was a new voice, and pure syrup. There was so much sugar in the tea it was sticky sweet.

'There, you see?' Mary scowled at me and took a step forward.

'Don't be daft – it's a con, as plain as puddin'.'

'Got any better ideas?' Before I knew it she had gripped the broken edges of the door and levered herself through the thin gap in the middle. Neither Mog nor me could have stopped her. But we were straight after her. Me clinging on to Mary, Mog clinging on to me.

Behind the door the sickly glowing light clung to the stone walls of a massive open space, kept itself to itself, lit up next to nothing. The space was a cavern, no, a great hall. There were stone pillars holding up a ceiling that was so high it was lost in the dark.

'Er. Hello . . .' Mary said, speaking to the

empty hall, 'HELLO! Is anybody here?' There were no bodies to put to the voices we'd heard. I tried to whistle, just to prove that I wasn't bothered, but it wouldn't come out properly.

'Pooh – something's dead in here,' Mog said, her nose twitching as she sniffed the air. 'Long dead too, by the whiff of it.' I tried to ignore her, and looked around. The floor was littered with tiny bits of coloured stone – what was left of a mosaic I think. And through a tiny window set high up in the bare wall a miserable ray of moonlight dribbled in. It was catching against the edges of a huge wooden table and chairs set out with bowls and goblets and stuff. Everything seemed to be broken, twisted out of shape with rot or damp. There was nothing else in the great hall. Well . . . At the far end, an odd half-shadow fell across the floor just where there was nothing to throw a shadow. I pretended not to notice that.

Mog jumped up onto the table and stuck her nose into one of the rough wooden bowls. There was something black and shrivelled and solid stuck to its insides. Cobwebs had long since settled on it. Dust had settled on the cobwebs. It was a meal someone had left in a hurry, and they hadn't come back. Mog pawed at the bowl in disgust, and turned her back on it.

'Well, have you seen enough yet? There's nobody here now,' I said. It was wishful thinking, I know. Mary didn't hear anyhow. She was jigging up and down with a lopsided, faraway look on her face – as if she was concentrating really, really hard. Too hard. I knew that look, and I couldn't believe it. I'd seen that look on buses and in cinema queues, on long summer walks, and even in the middle of Gran's funeral. It was Mary's *I know it's not a very good time, but I really do need to go to the bog* kind of look, *and if I don't go this instant there's going to be one heck of an accident.*

'Oh no, not now, Mary,' I said.

'There must be one around here somewhere – I'm bursting,' she said, her face twisting painfully.

'Just think about something else,' I said. I've never read a book yet where kids go off on adventures and stuff and have to stop right in the middle just to go to the bog. Not once, not even if they're away for months.

'I can't think about anything else,' she said.

'Well, cross your legs or stick a bung in it.'

'I'm tellin' on you, Billy Tibbet.' This wasn't the right place for an argument and it might have gone on forever if something hadn't stopped it stone dead.

The shadow against the back wall moved.

Mary was tugging at me now. 'Look, Billy,' she said. But she didn't need to – I was looking.

There were three figures, huddled together against the wall, but what there was of them wasn't enough to make even one. You see, I could see right through them, like a jelly on a plate. Their thin pale skin hardly caught the light at all.

'Billy . . . Billy, they're like . . .'

'Ghosts!' Mog finished, her hair standing out as straight as the bristles on a broom. You could have tied her to the end of a stick and swept the floor with her. The funny thing was, though, I don't know who was the more frightened – us or them.

'I'm *so* sorry if we scared you.' It was the

same coaxing, sickly sweet voice we'd heard before.

'Boodies didn't *mean* to,' said another.

'Boodies *very* sorry.' As the voices spoke, they melted slowly together. 'Can't be *too* careful.'

'Couldn't have known.'

'Didn't realise.'

I tried not to listen. Tried to hold on tight to Mary. But there were more and more voices. Not three now. On the chairs, on the table. All around the walls. And then behind us, blocking our way to the door.

'Poor, poor Billy. Poor Mary.'

'So tired . . . tired of carrying silly little books.'

The book. *The book.* Oh, Billy Tibbet, you flamin' daft divvy.

'Billy, I'm frightened,' Mary said. Cold twists of air wrapped themselves around us. A singing wind growing fingers. Fingers and hands, with a touch lighter than a feather's stroke and colder than ice. We were being pulled apart.

'No. No. NO!' I could see Mog's tail flashing angrily. She was trying to get to Mary. Mary?

She seemed so far away from me. I called out.

'The book. Open the book, sis.' She had to open it. The book would help. The wind snatched the words right out of my mouth and howled louder. 'Bones and blood,' it sang, 'bones and blood.'

And then, right in the middle of it all, I heard someone laughing. Really. A huge great belly laugh, like my dad's when he's watching daft comics on the telly. That was when something smashed through the door, breaking it into a billion tiny little bits. It was all arms and legs, grabbing and grasping. Great bucket-and-spade hands chomping out lumps of floor and wall, cracking stone pillars as easy as Blackpool rock.

It was Grundiggar, the rock troll.

The singing winds turned to squeaks and squeals, and cries of blue murder. Boodies were everywhere and nowhere all at once. Oozing in and out of cracks in the stonework in a desperate effort to get away. But there was no getting away. Another big grey wall of a figure lurched through the broken doorway, and in a strange lolloping dance tore away three of the stone pillars at a go. And then there was Mog, madly slashing and clawing. Boodies slipping through her paws, thin as an oil leak, squawking as they went. 'Don't hurt the boodies! . . . *Poor* little boodies! . . . Done no harm.'

I joined in the fight. Me and Mary both. Clambered up onto the table and stood a good pitch while we had it. But we didn't really have the knack of fighting boodies. The air was choked up with clouds of eye-stinging muck, plaster and bits of stone and stuff. It would have been easier to tie knots in running water.

'Roof's coming down!' Someone cried out. The tall central pillar buckled, cracked and twisted apart.

'Get out, Mary,' I yelled. But the last I saw of her she was falling, disappearing behind a storm of dust, screams, flying fists and chair legs. I remember moving, dragged, I think. Then, for a dark instant, nothing else.

A bang on the ear. That's what did it. A falling stone maybe, or a wild swing from a heavy grey arm off its mark. Anyway, seconds later I was somehow outside, head spinning like a top, and staggering around punch-drunk trying to stay on my feet. I could see the moon low in the sky, its big worried face staring down at me. Then there were two faces.

'Not a flattened Tibbet then is it?' said Grundiggar, and I was sure one of his black nail-head eyes gave a wink.

'Er, no. No.' At least I didn't think so. I was still trying to decide where I was. Still giddy. There was no more screaming. No shouts or anything, dust in the air. No boodies. There were trees and bushes though – with leaves too! And there were lines and lines of stones running all over the ground, marking out the walls of buildings like a map. Or rather, like an old ruin. Here and there, narrow banks of grass had grown up over the fallen stones. I know that much – I fell over one. Face first. When I picked myself up again Mog was standing looking at me. There was blood on her fur.

'Where's Mary?' I asked, anxious. Mog turned away self-consciously, licked her wound. Grundiggar, standing behind her, lifted his arm and, looking more than a little bit worried, scratched his head.

'I'm here, Billy.' The voice came first, then the legs and then the rest of her, straight out of the bushes.

'But sis, I saw you fall. I was sure . . . I thought—'

'I didn't fall, I jumped. Had to. Couldn't hang on another second.'

'What?'

'*I said*, didn't I?'

'Eh?'

'*I said* – the bog, Billy. The bog.' I didn't know whether to clobber her or cuddle her. The great rock troll took a deep breath and guffawed with laughter.

We spent the whole of that night with the rock trolls. In among the ruins. I remember the moon dropping behind the trees, getting lost in the distant mountains. And as it went the whole world turning black again. Mary nearly jumping out of her skin when the bushes around us suddenly shimmered with their own light. Every leaf a tiny flame. It was an odd old place.

Mary and me sat with Mog at the top of a

grassy bank. By the light of the bushes we watched Grundiggar and Bruggle gathering great armfuls of rock. They picked their way carefully between the lines of fallen stone walls, just as if they were doing their weekly shop at the local supermarket. The small'uns followed along behind them and copied.

'You'd better tell them we can't eat that stuff,' Mary said under her breath. 'There's a hole inside me the size of our house, but I am not eating rocks.'

Mog flicked her tail in silent agreement. I didn't know how to tell them.

'We're guests,' I said limply.

Grundiggar guffawed with laughter and broke a stone open in his hand, as easy as cracking a nut. He picked out what he thought were the good bits, and gave us a handful each. Even our Mog got some. The small'uns stuffed the whole lot into their mouths in one go – as a sort of sign of encouragement.

'Manners,' said Bruggle, politely popping the tiniest piece of rock into her mouth. Well, in the end we did eat it, and . . . and it was flamin' awful. A mouthful of soil doesn't even come close. Worse than anything the Stringers had been trying to poison us with. There was a drink to go with it, too, and that was worse than worse. Wrung out of a tree trunk and passed around in huge scooped-out pieces of bark. I'm not going to describe the taste because it would only make you sick.

The only good bit of that meal came right at the very end, *after* we'd finished eating. Just as we began to fall asleep . . . the rock trolls began to sing. It started with a sort of thrumming noise. A gentle low sound, deep in their throats. Then there were words.

The small'uns sang first. They sang about daft things. About flying dragons . . . and wierd magical pools . . .

And then, Bruggle sang. She sang about the crumbling mountain left behind us at the bottom of the invisible stairs, and how they had followed us up the stairs to safety. She sang about the great battle at the boodies den, and how silly it had been of us to go messing about with the likes of boodies in the first place.

And then, last of all, Grundiggar began to sing, and his songs were sad. He sang about

75

things I didn't really understand, about the end of the Spellbinders . . . about the misery that was the fall of a world called Murn . . . about the poor rock trolls left to wander homeless across a wasted world . . . He even sang about the book, and Murdle Clay, and began to tell us how to go about finding him . . . and, and he . . . and my eyes were shutting without me telling them to . . .

'Mary . . . you listening to this? You still awake?'

When we woke up it was morning, and the moon was back in the sky. The rock trolls had gone on their way.

EIGHT

The Stairs Down

Strained silence.

'I thought you were listening,' I said.

'Well, I thought *you* were listening,' Mary said.

'I was asleep.'

'*I* was asleep.'

We both looked down at our Mog. She was curled up on her back, and if one eye had been peering at us slyly it was snapped shut again.

Strained silence.

'You must remember some of what they said. I don't see why I should be stuck out here. Right in the middle of nowhere. I didn't start all this, Billy.'

Strained silence.

'We'd better have something to eat,' I said, more to change the subject than anything. The rock trolls had left us a small pile of eating stones. A kind of present.

'And I'm not having any more of that rotten

stuff, either,' Mary said.

'There's nothing else,' I said.

Strained silence.

In the end we were both nibbling half-heartedly. Better a mouth-too-full-to-speak silence than an awkward brooding one. What a sight we must have looked. Bashed, scraped, crumpled, not the lick of a wash for days. Out all night. *And* sleeping in our clothes – they never ever felt comfortable again. Itched in all the wrong places.

'Here,' Mary flung the book at me. 'You try and open it again. I'm sick of tugging at the useless thing.'

'You be more careful with that,' I said. 'And anyway, I've tried a million times and it won't open.' Mary just scowled.

'Well, try a million and one.'

'I thought the ruddy thing was meant to help us when we needed it,' I shouted, my voice sounding more brittle and hard than I really meant. I suppose I was angry – at myself, at Mary, at the book too.

I was sure somehow we were in the right place. The rock trolls hadn't left us in among the ruins by accident, and the book had got something to do with it. It wanted us there. It was all part of the PLEASE RETURN bit, all part of us finding Murdle Clay.

Strained silence.

'Maybe it already has,' Mog said at last, giving herself a long slow stretch.

'What?' Mary and me said together. Puzzled.

Mog carefully licked clean the wound in her side before she answered. 'Maybe the book already has given us help.'

I looked at Mary – she was trying to think. 'Stairs,' she said. 'It gave us stairs, Mog. And we've used them. Up and down stairs. That's all.'

'No,' said Mog, with the beginnings of an I-know-something-you-don't-know smirk on her face. 'No, it didn't – it gave us stairs up and stairs down.'

'That's what I just said.'

'No, not stairs up and stairs down. Stairs up *and* stairs down. *Two flights of stairs!*' Two flights of stairs. The answer had been there all the time, poking us in the eye.

'Mog – I could kiss you.' Mary lunged and

Mog scooted before the damage could be done.

'Right – come on then,' I said. This was more like it. 'We're getting out of here.'

'Er . . . haven't you forgotten something?' Mary said.

'Er?'

'We don't know where the stairs are, do we?'

Mog was giving me one of her looks, waiting for me to work that one out. I already had. 'We do. Don't you remember? Mog said it herself. All we've got to do is sort of believe in the stairs and they'll be there – right where we want them to be.'

'All right then, smart Alec – where's the stairs around here? We want stairs to go down. Can't go walking in thin air this time, and all I can see are trees and bushes and bits of rock.' Mary was getting annoyed again. 'There's no cracks or secret doors, no holes in the ground. No way to go down stairs at all.'

Another knowing look from Mog, and then she got ready to perform her party trick, just like she had done at the STAIRS UP. First, she snuffled around a bit between the lines of fallen stones. If they really had been the walls of buildings then there had been floors between them. And if there had been floors there might just have been cellars or, or something. She stopped at a small bump in the ground, gave us a quick look as if to say this was it, and then with a short hop she launched herself. Not up, but down. Down. Straight into the ground. Just as if she was tripping down a flight of stairs.

'But, but . . .' Mary stuttered.

'Go on then, you're next,' I said.

'You're not getting me down there – walking through the ground. Where does that take us, Billy?' I wish she hadn't asked that. That was the one flaw in the plan, the one niggle, and I didn't know the answer.

'Out of here – that's where,' I said quickly. 'Just shut your eyes and get on with it. I'll be right behind you.' I gave her a push to get her moving, before she had time to think about it. She shut her eyes, and tottered forward.

'There really, really, are stairs here . . . and if there aren't, Billy Tibbet, I'm going to clobber—' She disappeared through the ground after Mog.

I was after Mary like a shot. I'd lost her too

many times already to lose her again. I didn't think about it, I just jumped. It was like . . . it was like . . . well, walking through solid ground isn't really like anything I can describe. There was wormy soil, bits of rocks, tree roots and that. But I passed straight through it all. Or maybe it passed through me, I don't really know which. I felt warm trickling shivers running up and down inside of me. Right inside. They were in my toes from the very first step, and the deeper I went the further they spread, until finally they came right out through the top of my head. Maybe it hurt too, really badly, but it was the kind of pain I didn't mind having. Daft, I know. Twisting a loose tooth right around just before it snaps out, or stamping hard on a newly-sprained foot just to make sure it's still agony – that was it. I kept going. Scrunched my eyes up tight shut until they hurt too. Felt my way down blind, and hoped it would end soon.

It did.

NINE

At the Bottom of the Stairs

'Where are we?'

Slowly, I opened my eyes. There was a light. The same sickly left-overs of yellow light that had hung about the walls of the boodies' den. Mary and Mog were standing next to me, as close as they could get.

We were in a tiny room, with stone walls that met an arched ceiling just above our heads. If I'd stood up on tip-toes, and spread my arms out wide I could have touched opposite walls *and* the ceiling – all at the same time. My legs were rolling, but not with dizziness. The floor we were standing on was loose and uneven. At first I couldn't see what it was made of, but Mary could.

'Billy I can hardly breathe.' Her voice crackled, thinner than toast. 'And I'm walking on lumps of . . . lumps of . . . *uurgh!* Lumps of bone, I can't put a foot down without standing on them.'

'Try to find the door,' I said, my chest tight and heaving as it pulled in the room's thin stale air.

'This room hasn't got a door,' she said. Next to her crackle there was an accusation in her voice. 'There isn't a door. The air's not meant for breathing. And there are bones everywhere.'

'What do you expect to find in a tomb?' Mog said matter-of-factly.

'A tomb!' Mary was jumping and kicking and squeaking. 'Well, that's it. That's it! I want to get out of here. Out now, Billy!' She began hopping and stomping and pulling wild faces in an effort to will herself out through the floor. She didn't go anywhere. Not this time. There were no more secret stairs to climb.

'I think we're here,' I said, snatching for breath.

'What do you mean, *here*?'

'Wherever the stairs were taking us, I suppose.'

'I don't care where they were taking us – it's a tomb, Billy. A rotten grave with bones and . . . *bones* . . .' Her face was going all the wrong sort of shapes. I couldn't stand it if she was going to blubber.

'Don't Mary. It might be a tomb – but it

doesn't feel much like a tomb, does it? I mean, it doesn't *feel* scary or anything.' That was the real puzzle, it didn't feel scary. It didn't feel exactly safe, just not scary. Mary stopped her ranting and tried to stand still without putting her feet on the floor.

'Well, no, no it doesn't, but *the smell* . . .'

'Huh! It doesn't beat Dad's socks after a day out in the garden. And at least there aren't any worms or maggots or—' I should have stopped while I was ahead.

'Try that rotten book again, Billy. Just you open that book.' I did. And this time the pages were flipping themselves open almost before I had my hand in my pocket, like the book was eager to get on. 'Well?' Mary asked impatiently. 'What does it say?'

'Er . . .' I hesitated. 'Idrik Sirk.'

'What?'

'It says *Idrik Sirk*. And that's all it says.'

'Idrik Sirk. What's that supposed to mean?'

'Well, I don't know, do I. Maybe it's a name or something.'

'A name – Idrik Sirk . . .' said Mog. 'Sounds more like a spelling mistake to me.'

'Oh, I'm fed up with stupid riddles. Are you sure that's all there is to it, Billy? Give me a proper look.' Mary would have snatched, if another voice hadn't spoken. A voice that sounded just like a cold draught howling down a dark empty passageway. A voice that came up at us from right beneath our feet.

'Ka! Of course Idrik Sirk is a name. It's my name. And will you *please* stop standing on me – can't you see the condition I'm in?' We leapt backwards, Mary and me both, landed smack-bang up against the wall.

'I'm not listening,' Mary said, sticking her fingers in her ears. 'I've just about had enough of all this tripe and anyway, since when can bones talk?'

'Since when can little girls walk through walls?' said Idrik Sirk. There was a grinding, scraping noise and he somehow managed to sit himself up. He wasn't just bits of bone. He was a skeleton. A whole one.

'You really dead, then?' Mog asked, giving him a sniff out of curiosity, before settling herself down in his lap. (Well, in what was left of his lap).

'Could be worse,' he answered vaguely. If he'd had a face I would have been able to tell whether he was scowling or smiling. He lifted his skull towards us and, letting it rock from side to side, gave us the once over. 'Well, you're not Spellbinders, that's for certain,' he said.

There was that word again – straight out of Grundiggar's song.

'Spell – whats-its?'

''Binders of spells, boy. Binders of spells,' he said, as if turning the words on their head explained everything. 'Don't know your wizards from your warlocks. Or your witches from your twitches by the look of you. Ka!' His might have been an empty face but the look he gave me then could have burned a hole in me. 'And that'll not belong to you either!' I felt myself sizzle red, like I'd been caught picking my nose or something. I was still holding the book open in my hand. I snapped it shut and stuffed it back into my pocket. Idrik Sirk lifted his bony hands as if to study them, clack-clacking one against the other. 'No, you're not 'Binders. But this is clever riddle-diddle. Not a fool's tinkering.' He paused for a moment. 'Stole it, did you?' he asked.

'No, I, we . . .' That was the trouble. I suppose technically I had stolen the book. But well, only from a thief, so that can't possibly count for anything, can it?

'Don't say *anything*, Billy!' Mary hissed at me.

Idrik Sirk ignored her remark. 'I was a Spellbinder myself, once. Aye, before . . . before I died.' He huffed and puffed a bit and, dropping his head onto one side, seemed to lose himself inside his thoughts. When at last he lifted his head again, he asked, 'What is it that you want, then?'

'Want?'

'Aye, boy. Aye, girl. You must have come bothering me for something. You, and this cat here.' The draughty note in his voice grew louder. 'Or are you in the habit of waking the dead for nothing?'

'No, no, we've never done it before,' I said.

'No, I don't expect you have, boy. Don't expect you have.'

'Just don't say *anything*,' Mary hissed again.

Maybe she was right. We were in a big enough
mess as it was. Maybe I could find a way to get
us out. We didn't need any help. But there was
something about this bloke, something I
couldn't rightly explain. And all of a sudden my
stomach's heavy as lead, and churning, tying
itself in knots, and I'm wanting him to take the
whole load off me. And if he's dead and just a
bunch of dry old bones it doesn't make any
difference. The story tumbled out, words
tripping over themselves in their rush to get
out of my mouth. I told him everything.
Everything. Beginning to end. You know it all
well enough by now. Idrik Sirk didn't say a
word, didn't move a musc— a bone, not until
I'd got to the bit where we landed up on top of
him in his own tomb.

Slowly, he eased himself to his feet, bending
himself almost double so as not to bang his
skull off the low ceiling. Then, with Mog
nestling in his arms, he clack- clacked his way
to the far side of the tomb. Like he'd been sent
to the corner for sniggering at the poetry in
one of Prissy Pringle's English lessons. I took
hold of Mary's hand, you know, just so she'd

know everything was all right. Then Idrik Sirk was huffing and puffing again, every breath an oh dear.

'Should have stayed well out of it, boy. Taking what's not yours. Fooling about in other folk's business. And yet, if what you say is true, then . . .' He rattled his fingers against his jaw bone, like he didn't dare repeat what he was really thinking and was fishing for something else to say instead. 'Do you, do you know what it is you've got there, in your pocket?'

'Well – er . . . it's just a book, isn't it?'

'Just. *Just*. It isn't *just* anything. Ka! What you've got there, boy, is a Twitch.'

'A *Twitch*?'

'Aye – a Spellbinder's Twitch. Can't have a Spellbinder without a Twitch. Nor a Twitch without a 'Binder. Had one myself when I was alive. Of course, I went in for a firestone, much simpler, and a lot less fiddle-faddle than a book. If you don't mind getting your fingers burnt now and then.'

'But what's a Twitch for, then?' Mary asked.

'What's it for? What's it for, girl? Ka! You'll be telling me next you don't know what your nose is for. Spellbinding's no tin-pot trade. Can't go picking it up in five minutes. Took me a hundred and fifty years, near enough, to learn what I learned. And where was I going to keep that amount of learning, you tell me that?'

'In . . . in your head,' I offered.

'Inside my head? You're worse than she is, boy. You can't go leaving that kind of learning stuffed inside a head – where it's bound to leak out all over the place. Mess and mayhem! No. You keep it in a Twitch, of course.'

'Oh, I see,' I said, nodding. And Mary nodded with me. But we didn't see, not really.

Idrik Sirk clack-clacked a finger against his skull. 'And think on this while you're about it, my little sneak-thieves. There are those who would do *murder* to get their hands upon the powers of a Twitch. Do murder, and think nothing of it.' He paused, and took a deep breath, for dramatic effect. 'And what do you go and do with yours? You walk right into a boodies' den. Ha, I would have liked to have seen that. Why not announce yourselves to the whole world? Here everybody, look what we've got. Anyone else want a look? Ka! Well, there's a problem you've got chasing your tails.'

'We didn't know!' Mary protested.

'No, you didn't know, girl. But not knowing's no excuse. Boodies won't let you go, not now they know what's up. And I hope you haven't brought any of the vile, nasty little creatures with you? I don't want them creeping about in here.' The way he spoke made me want to scratch all over.

'No. We haven't,' Mary said, squirming around inside her dress, looking for extra pockets she hadn't got, just in case.

'If you've got a spare hole in a button they'll be in there biding their time. Waiting their chance. Ka . . . mucking about with boodies and rock trolls!'

'The trolls were on our side!' Mary snapped.

'Sides. *Our* side. So, you think there are sides, do you? The goodies and the baddies? The right and the wrong? And me, whose side am I on? Yours? Theirs? Or my own, maybe? Ka! There are no sides. Not here. Not any more. It's too late for sides. You'll learn that – one way or the other, girl, you'll learn.'

'Well, cheer us up, why don't you!' There

was a sting in her voice that caught as a tear.

'And it's too late to cry,' he said. But his words weren't thrown out this time. No, softer than soft. 'Didn't know a thing. I don't suppose you even know where you are?'

'No,' I shouted. Sure that we didn't. 'No, we don't. And we don't want to know an' all. We just want to give Murdle Clay his book back. We want to find the Stringers. And we want to go home.'

Idrik Sirk's bony fingers slowly stroked Mog's fur coat. He was considering something. 'Ah yes, well . . . If only it was that simple. What have you seen here, boy? Eh, girl? What have you seen?' His voice was still annoyingly quiet. I was still shouting.

'Seen? Well, mountains. Loads and loads of flippin' mountains—'

'And old ruins,' said Mog.

'And dried-up dead trees, and earthquakes,' said Mary.

'Murn,' said Idrik Sirk, slowly. 'That is where you are. Murn, with her ninety-seven mountains . . . whereupon dwelt one 'Binder each.' He brightened for a moment, before suddenly remembering something really horrible and slumping back into misery. 'Or rather – what's left of Murn, that is.'

'Billy Tibbet, if you think I'm climbing ninety-seven mountains, even to find the Stringers, you've got a hole in your head,' Mary said. Idrik Sirk wasn't listening.

'No, there's not much left of this world. Murn's not what it was. Not since it was struck.'

'Struck?' I said.

'Aye, struck down! Murn was the greatest spell of them all. 'Binders saw to that. Oh, you should have seen it. That was *real* magic.

'Great mountain cities that no earthly fashioned stones could ever equal. The sparkle of the crying rivers, that ran forever with tears of joy. The broad forest-orchards giving bounty enough for all who hungered. And, above all these things, the ring of careless laughter – the sound of true freedom . . .' He hesitated, and dropped Mog to the floor, as if the burden he was carrying inside was already too much for him. 'But then . . . the flame that gives the greatest light also casts the longest shadow.

Look about you. *Look!* Light and dark. There's never one without the other. Never. And from the shadow came jealousy . . . Ka!

'But that's another's tale, for other ears, not yours. I will tell you only this – there were sides then, oh yes, there were sides then all right. 'Binder turned upon 'Binder . . . and in league with the greatest of all thieves, the greatest of all liars—' At last he stopped, but without finishing.

'Billy, I don't understand,' Mary whispered. 'I don't.'

Why is it that grown-ups, even dead skeleton grown-ups, always talk in riddles. Nothing's said properly. So you have to figure it all out for yourself. Well, I could figure it out. I'd finish his story for him. 'Mary,' I said. 'What he means is – the Spellbinders have been fighting each other. Fighting, like in a war, killing each other and that. And now, because of it, their whole world's falling to bits. Y'know, just like you get on the telly.'

'Did – did the wrong side win then?' she asked. It wasn't a daft question, but Idrik Sirk suddenly laughed. It wasn't a funny laugh.

'You still don't understand, do you?' he said. He shook his head miserably. 'There are no winners. There can never be winners. Murn is ninety-seven, but it is also one. When any world turns upon itself, how can there be winners? There is desolation. There is waste. And finally . . . there is an end.' His bony fingers gestured towards himself as if to prove his point. 'Without the 'Binders the light of Murn goes out. It is as well that you have seen but a small part. Upon the mountains mischief, selfishness, greed, and all the creatures of the dark, walk freely. The shadow spreads. Soon it will be finished. Forever.'

Huh, whatever happened to fairytale princesses and happy endings?

'Billy, does that mean that all the Spell-binders are dead then?' Mary said, her face twisted up, desperately trying to understand.

'Well, yes—' I said . . . but then I changed my mind. 'No. No it doesn't.' I turned to Idrik Sirk. 'You – you said there can't be a Twitch without a Spellbinder. Not one without the other. And we've got a Twitch. So . . . so Murdle Clay can't be dead, can he? And he's a Spellbinder. And,

and if he's alive, then maybe Murn *can* be saved after all?'

It was a very long time before Idrik Sirk spoke again, and when he did he was talking to himself. 'Aye, well . . . *Please return this book*, that was the first. Aye . . . *and help save*, that was the second . . . Maybe those who have lived so long aren't that easily killed. Older than the dragons, 'Binders are, older than Murn itself, older than the dead maybe . . .'

'Well – where is he then?' Mary snapped.

Idrik Sirk sighed. Sighed as if he was carrying the whole world on his back. 'I don't know. My memory is only distant whispers now. And of Murdle Clay I remember nothing.

'At the very end did he cast the spell of exile, rather than wait upon a certain death?' He turned his empty face towards us pleadingly. 'And if he did, what choice is that to a 'Binder? To run from this, our world, into another. Ka! Death or death it might as well be. You see, boy, you see, girl, in the weaving of the exile spell is bound the thread of forgetfulness. Forgetfulness. Deeper even than a 'Binder's dream . . .'

'Oh, well, that's just great,' I said. 'Murdle Clay doesn't even know that he's Murdle Clay. And, he could be anywhere. So we've got about as much chance of finding him as me dad's got of winning the flippin' pools.'

'Ka! Don't give up so fast, boy,' said Idrik Sirk. 'The spells bound within that Twitch of yours didn't find their own way there. There's maybe more to this than even I can explain.'

'Well, what about Jenny Haniver, can you explain her?' Mary blurted out. 'Did she chase after him or something? You know, to pinch his Twitch?'

'Eh? Jenny Haniver – chased? Ka!' Idrik Sirk sounded first flustered, then annoyed. 'You try my patience, girl.'

'Well, I like that!' said Mary. 'She's got to fit into this somehow, and I only said—'

'Jenny Haniver is *not* from Murn, child.'

'But—'

'Boggart, demon, hag or bogeyman, call her what you will – this Jenny Haniver is from your own world.'

'But that's impossible,' she cried. 'Things like that are made up. They're just pretend where we come from. They're not *real*.'

'Not real!' His bones rattled and clacked. He was laughing, and it was real laughter this time. 'Ha ha! Not real she says. I can just see the kind of mess that's left behind you at home. Ha! Well, that's a can of worms that'll have to keep. That's no trouble of mine.'

His words swept around us, hitting harder than driving rain in a thunderstorm. For an instant I was back in the Stringers' kitchen. There was Jenny Haniver, with her curdled smile and dry-stick breath. She was trying to pull the book out of my hand. And the lasses were there, Swot, Lippy Jane, Conk and Sprog, clinging on to me the best they could, locked in a mad, desperate struggle. I'd told Idrik Sirk the tale, them included, but from the moment I'd left them in that kitchen I'd hardly given them a thought. Not really.

Idrik Sirk had stopped laughing. He looked suddenly very, very tired. His head rolled slowly to one side, like he'd had enough. Like whatever was keeping all his bits together in one piece was about to give way.

'Billy . . .' Mary was getting ready to explode

again. 'This whole thing just keeps getting worse, and worse, *and worse*!'

'Can't you do anything?' I asked Idrik Sirk.

'What do you expect me to do, boy?'

'I don't know,' I said.

'I'm dead, you know. Stone dead. And dead men stay where dead men lie.'

'Well, it was your name that was in the book,' Mog said. She sprang to her feet and swished her tail at him. 'That must count for something.'

'Aye, well—' He wandered through his thoughts again. 'Maybe this cat's got more sense than the rest of us put together.'

Idrik Sirk lifted his arms and gently rested them around our shoulders. It helped. Just bones I know, dead bones, but it did help.

'If I'd been alive, then I could have found you your Murdle Clay. 'Binder can't hide from 'Binder – wherever they are. It's just that—'

'It's just that you're not alive,' Mary interrupted, 'you're dead, and dead men thingy thingy thingy – like you said.'

'There might be a way,' he said cautiously.

'What way?' I said.

'Murdle Clay's Twitch . . . the book.'

'You want us to give you the book?' I cried, pulling myself free of his arm.

He didn't answer.

'Billy, this whole rotten world could drop to pieces at any minute. If Idrik Sirk really was a Spellbinder, you know, when he was alive, then maybe he can help,' Mary said. 'And I really do want to go home.'

'But, how do we know we can trust you?' I said, staring straight into the empty eye sockets of his skull.

'You don't,' he said flatly.

After all the trouble we'd been through, and all the stuff he'd spouted, who'd have thought I would have just handed the book over to him? Well I did, as easy as that.

The second he took it, Murdle Clay's little book didn't look quite the same. Sort of newer for one thing, and well, different. And the way it opened up for him it could have been any old book you like. There was a real purpose, even a pleasure, in the way he pored over it. His fingers ran happily down the edges of the pages. Puzzling over invisible indexes,

101

searching out the ghosts of chapter headings, flicking eagerly backwards and forwards.

Finally, reluctantly, he found his way to the page he was looking for. There his fingers lingered. And lingered . . . And then at last, he turned the book so that we could all see it.

There was a picture. A picture of a blue mountain. And that was all really. Not because there wasn't any more detail. No, it's just that it wasn't what was in that picture that mattered, rather it was the way the picture felt. Yes, felt.

'Escareth,' Idrik Sirk said simply. 'The mountain of Escareth.'

'Is it in Murn?' I asked. He nodded.

'Oh Billy, it's so sad . . .' said Mary. It was the saddest picture in the whole world and we didn't know why.

An instant later, and it wasn't a picture in a book any more. There was a hard wind blowing across my face, and the air was so fresh my lungs burned with the sudden shock of breathing it. I heard Mary call out, 'Will we see you again?' And I heard the daft, stupid answer.

'Do pigs fly?'

Then Mary was at my side. Mog too, standing right up to her body in long blue grass with the book held between her teeth.

Below us, miles below us, were the tops of distant mountains. Behind us, with its head stuck so far above everything else it got lost in the sky, was a huge wall of rock. A mountain as blue as a Smartie.

There was no Idrik Sirk.

TEN

Watchers and Watched

I noticed it from the start – an odd feeling –
from the moment I found myself standing
among the blue grass. It was uncomfortable
and creepy. Like we were being secretly
watched. Like there were eyes, lots of eyes,
staring. Like the whole mountain was staring. I
tried turning my head quickly in the direction
of the watchers. There was nothing there. A
few scattered rocks, a tree leaning against the
wind. A twist of grass. Nothing. But they had
been there the instant before I looked. And
they would be there again the instant I turned
away. I tried to shrug it off, didn't say anything.

Mary was sitting among the grass. The wind
blew her hair back – there were tears on her
face. She was staring at the endless stack of
mountains spread out below us. The ninety-
seven mountains of Murn. Each peak was a
flash of colour among a brilliant patchwork of
colour. Or at least, they should have been. Here

and there the colours had become thin and watery. And some weren't colours at all, now. Just grey, or black. I'd seen that look before. Maybe a whole world really can die. Huh. Didn't seem fair somehow.

The moon was up in the sky. It looked more worried than ever.

'Mary – are you all right?' I said.

'Idrik Sirk knew, didn't he,' she said. 'He knew he couldn't come with us to Escareth. He had to stay down there, in that – that horrible place. On his own – dead.' There was no fathoming our Mary sometimes. Ten minutes ago, when we'd been stuck in that tomb with him, she'd been wanting to bite his head off.

'I don't know. Maybe,' I said. Maybe I wasn't really listening. My ears were somewhere else. With the watchers. With the blue mountain of Escareth.

'Billy, do you think we'll ever get home?'

'I'll tell you what I think,' I said, talking too loudly, letting the wind carry my voice, almost wanting the watchers to hear. 'None of this is an accident. Right from the flippin' start. I think Murdle Clay wanted us here, in Escareth.

Showed us the stairs. Showed us Idrik Sirk, even. He wants his book back, and when he gets it I think he really is going to try and save Murn.'

Mog was sitting next to Mary, the book was still in her mouth. Her ears twitched alert, and she let it drop to the ground. As it fell the wind changed, its push became a pull, as sharp as a drawn breath. But a mountain can't gasp, can it?

Mog gave the air a sniff. 'I wish he'd just tell us where he is, so we can find him.' She nudged the book with her nose. It didn't fly open. Glued tight shut again.

'Well, if Idrik Sirk was right, and this is Escareth, then he's here somewhere,' I said. 'So maybe we've found him already?' I let my voice grow louder with every word, sure that the eyes were still there, still watching.

'So, what do we do now?' Mary asked. 'We can't just sit here for ever.'

Huh! I didn't know. Maybe we were waiting for the watchers, or the mountain, or Murdle Clay even. Waiting for them to *do* something. I couldn't tell them that. I took the book away from Mog, shoved it inside my shirt – like I knew what I was doing – and said the first thing that came into my head.

'I don't know about you two, but I'm parched.' I know it wasn't much of an answer, but when I thought about it for a second it was suddenly true. We'd had nothing to drink since our stone dinner with the rock trolls, and that was yesterday. 'I'll probably die of thirst if we don't find something in the next five minutes,' I said. That's the trouble with stuff like thirst, once you start thinking about it you can't think about anything else. Forget all about funny feelings and staring eyes. And the idea was contagious. All three of us were up on our feet and looking.

To one side of us, the plains of blue grass seemed to run on forever, only stopping when they smacked up against the blue mountain itself. It was only on the other side, to the right, that lumps of jagged blue stone punctured the grass, and bits of withered blue tree were scattered everywhere – too dead to hold their roots in the ground. It was from this side that the wind began to carry a noise I knew. The rush and clack of water . . .

'I can hear it,' Mary cried through panting breath. 'It's not far – just over there.' We'd started off walking, moving carefully, but we were running wildly now, it seemed so very important to get there. The sound came loudest from a thin crack, sliced as clean as a knife cut, through a massive upright slab of rock. The gap was just wide enough for my feet if I squished them up together. I tried to look into it, but there was nothing to see. Its sides closed up in the dark somewhere out of sight. Only when I looked up could I see a thin gash of light where the top of the rock touched the sky's edge.

'Funny kind of water,' Mog said. For all the noise we could hear, the few drips of water trickling out at the bottom could have been coming from a leaky tap. She sniffed, dabbled her paw in it, and walked away disgusted. I made a scoop of my hands and let the dribbles make a small blue puddle in it. Even the water was blue. I mean really blue, like paint.

'Can you drink it?' Mary asked. 'Hurry up and try – I'm gagging.'

'Hang on – we've got to be–' I dipped my tongue into it '–careful.' I didn't drink any more. Suddenly I was lost, wandering alone inside the oddest dream. I was a million miles away from anywhere – but somehow still there, still wide-awake, still with Mog and Mary.

The eyes of the mountain grew large then. The rocks began to twist, to turn and bend. They became more than rocks. Bits of ruined buildings. Then whole buildings. And then something like a city, noisy and alive with people and everything. Where the grass plains had been a weak mix of pale blues, new colours splashed by the bucket load. Rich forest greens and the reds and yellows and oranges of an orchard. And suddenly, right in the middle of it all, there was a river.

As quickly as it grew up, it all fell away again. The river. The city. The forest. It shrivelled up, back to nothing.

I felt my arms falling to my sides and heard the splash of water.

'Look,' someone screamed. In my dreams I was playing silly beggars, with make-believe

109

cities and that. And now, now I was making up monsters.

It towered over us, its massive head held high and proud, its body even bigger than the biggest of the rocks it was standing on. The rocks we were standing under. I couldn't think, could only stand and stare. Dumb. Like my mouth had been zipped shut. There was the heat of a fire and a roar of flame, and then steam frothed from its mouth. Hissing and spitting. Two burning red eyes stared down at us. Its wings, as big as a ship's sails, slashed through the air as they beat. And there were legs, fifteen, twenty – how many? – too many. And a tail . . . a dragon's tail.

A dragon.

A dragon that could speak.

'Shoo, shoo, get away from here – it's not safe,' it said in a very nervous undragon-like voice. 'Go on, shoo, go away.' Mary and Mog began to move just as the dragon's head stooped towards them.

'Yes, yes, run,' I wanted to shout out loud, 'run away from it.' And they did run. But they didn't run away from it. They ran towards it.

Mary charged at it with a stone in one hand and a stick in the other. Waving. Shouting. Using words I didn't even think she knew (and worthy of Mam's wash-your-mouth-out-with-soap routine). For a moment I was sure she was going to bash the dragon on the head with her stick. She was. She did. It was plain daft. You can't go fighting dragons with sticks and stones. Not even in a dream. As she hit it a second time the dragon suddenly burst apart. Its twenty pairs of legs ran off in twenty different directions all at the same time. Its flames fizzled out, and its wings crumpled up, flumping to the ground like so many pieces of a broken kite. There was a clang, clang, clang, and the dragon's huge black head clattered against the rocks, splashing boiling hot water everywhere as it went.

With the last clang I was jolted awake. Pulled out of my strange dream into a reality that was almost the same. Almost. I could see an upside-down iron pot, the remains of a fire, and tatters of black cloth blowing in the wind. The dragon wasn't part of my dream at all. And worse – it wasn't a real dragon either! The whole thing was a rotten trick. A lousy great big fake, made up out of milk bottle tops and plastic margarine tubs for the school play, or as good as. And it had taken me in, all the way down to my socks.

Pieces of the fake dragon were still running across the hillside. Mary and Mog were chasing after them, but they were losing the race. And then, as I watched, one piece of dragon lost its footing, stumbled and fell. I saw Mog lunge and pounce, and lunge and pounce. Mary followed her down. Between them they had caught themselves a pair of the fake dragon's legs.

'Hold on, Mary,' I yelled, skittering across the rocks and grass as fast as I could. I hit the struggling heap of bodies just as Mary shoved her handkerchief into a screeching hole. This dragon's legs had a mouth!

'Wgfn Mgfny,' the bundle beneath us pleaded. It took all three of us sitting on top of him to hold him down. And it *was* a him. Besides two legs there was a body, a pair of arms and a head. He was only half the size of Mary, but if we'd had to face him on our own I'm sure he would have been a match for any of us. His skin was rough and dry to touch and his body felt hard and knotted, the same way a tree trunk feels when you're climbing up it. I half-expected him to be blue too. He wasn't – more a sort of sicky-green colour – although that might have been because we were sitting on his stomach.

'Right,' I said, not really sure what we were supposed to do next, 'we want some straight answers.' Now it's odd, but when you've captured your enemy and have him just where you want him, it's really, really hard to think up good questions to ask.

'What – what's your name?' That was the best I could come up with.

'Wgfn Mgfny,' our prisoner muffled through the handkerchief.

'Eh?'

'Wgfn Mgfny,' he muffled again.

'I think we should take *that* out of his mouth now, Billy,' Mog said.

'Er . . . Well, er, Wug-uf-in Mug-uf-in-ee, I'm going to take the hanky out of your mouth now – but you've got to promise not to make a noise or . . . or . . .' (I couldn't think up a good *or*) 'or else,' I said.

'Wgfn Mgfny,' said Wgfn Mgfny.

I took hold of the hankerchief and pulled. I could have been setting off the school fire alarm. 'AaaARGH HELP! *Murder!* MURDER!' The hankerchief was stuffed straight back in again, along with clumps of blue grass and handfuls of loose dirt. It shut him up again, but if anyone was listening the damage was already done.

For an age we didn't move, just lay deathly quiet. But the other legs of the fake dragon didn't come stomping back to help.

I had to think again. 'Look, we're not going to murder you, but if you make a noise like that again we'll . . . we'll . . .'

'We'll *spellbind* you,' Mary finished, sure that this threat would do the trick. She was wrong. Wgfn Mgfny heaved up and down, his contorting face a mix-up between tearful and screaming blue murder. And then, all of a sudden it was us who were feeling guilty. Huh! I mean, what had we done? It wasn't us who had been trying to scare the living daylights out of people with fake dragons. I managed to get most of the soggy mess out of his mouth, and moving together, very slowly, we let him sit up. He didn't yell out this time, didn't run away.

'We're very sorry . . .' I said, trying to sound as if I meant it. I looked around at the others for some kind of help. Wgfn Mgfny was still heaving up and down, but at least the effect was a silent one. 'We aren't going to spellbind you or, or anything,' I said hopefully. 'We can't, because we're not Spellbinders. We're just travellers. Just an ordinary boy and girl, and a cat.' Mary and Mog nodded in furious agreement. Wgfn Mgfny heaved one last time, and settled down to glare at us.

'You say something to him, Mary,' I said.

'Like – like what?'

'Something friendly, y'know, something . . . nice.' She gave me a sidelong glance that was anything but nice and put on her best Sunday teatime face.

'You're an elf, aren't you?' she guessed.

'Elf!' He took a deep breath and shuffled himself about inside his clothes like he was searching for something he'd lost. 'Who's she calling elf?' The way he rolled his tongue

115

around inside his mouth I was sure he was
going to spit the word back at her.

'Oh, er . . . a goblin, then,' Mary guessed again.

'GOBLIN!' He did spit at her this time.
'GOBLIN!' He spat again. 'First she chases folk
with her sticks and stones. Then sets on them
with her gang of ruffians. And *then* – goes
scarin' them, makin' threats of magic and
callin' them GOBLIN.' He was ready to spit
again. Mary was feeling for her stick. I stuck
myself between them to stop another battle.

'Huh! From what I could see it was you who
was trying to scare us,' I said.

'We weren't tryin' to scare you,' he said
huffily, folding his arms across his chest.

'Oh yes you were!' Mary snapped.

'Weren't.'

'Were.'

'WEREN'T!'

'WERE!'

'We weren't scarin'. We were warnin'.'

'Warning? Well, dressing up like a rotten
dragon doesn't seem much like warning to
me!' Mary said.

'Well, it was. We're snooks and that's what

snooks do,' he said poking his nose so close to Mary's they nearly touched. 'We warn people. Warn them off. You don't know much about Escareth – about the blue mountain – do you?' He twisted his head around and poked his nose at me. 'It's not the kind of place for ordinary travellers, isn't this. That is, if folks really are what folks say they are.' He looked as if he was ready to spit again.

'We were thirsty,' I said. I didn't want to lie, but I didn't want to tell him anything either. 'We were only looking for a drink of water.'

'Well, you're better thirsty than—' He stopped himself, and looked down at the ground as if he was searching there for an easier word. 'You can't go drinkin' water that's touched,' he said.

'Touched?'

'First sip's for dreamin', second sip's for mirth, third sip's a nightmare, fourth sip's a curse.'

I was beginning to catch on. If all I'd had was the dream then I would hate to meet the nightmare.

'But what's the water touched with?' Mary asked.

Wgfn Mgfny frowned and gave a sigh. 'Some's touched for the good, most's touched for the bad, but it's all touched. Everything that grows, everything that doesn't. The whole mountain. It's all the same.'

'Yes, but touched by what?' Mary wouldn't let go.

'Well there's an ancient tale I could tell,' he said quietly, his voice almost solemn, 'of spilt magic . . . Spellbinder's magic.' And there he stopped again, and stared at us hard, sure that this would be enough to scare away our curiosity. My mind was racing so fast I don't think I ever caught it up again.

'Then – then there really are Spellbinders here?' I said.

'Were . . .' he said slowly, as if he wasn't keen to say any more.

'Were?'

'There's them that says it was upon Escareth the 'Binders fought their last battle. Fought and fell. Casting spell against spell. A clash that brought their final downfall and near tore the world apart.

'There's them that says that at the end, those

not counted among the dead simply fled. Disappeared up their own puffs of smoke. Murn was left with wounds so deep it will never be mended – not without the 'Binder's turn.

'So Escareth waits, and watches, and hopes – or at least, there's them that says . . .'

'And the spilt magic?' Mog asked, intrigued by it all.

'Like old iron, battle shield or sword, left where it fell. Old spells used and unused – spells too powerful to be wielded in anger. Wherever you walk in Escareth, the ground will never be clean of them.'

'So, you're not *really* expecting the Spellbinders to come back, then?' Mary asked innocently.

The snook rolled his tongue around the inside of his mouth and spat out a laugh. 'Ha! Don't go filling your heads with daft old stories. This mountain's got a bellyfull of poisons that's all.' He was laughing, but his eyes never left us, like they were searching, desperately searching for a secret.

What else could I do? I took Murdle Clay's

book out of my pocket and held it up. Wgfn Mgfny didn't move, didn't say a word. Just looked. That look was enough.

'Can you take us to him?' I said.

'There's them that says a 'Binder's Twitch can find its own way home . . .' He poked his nose at Mary, and then at me. 'The winds of Escareth have changed, and the mountain talks of magic in hushed whispers. Whispers are hope, but not meat and bone . . . No . . . No, I cannot find your 'Binder for you. But I will help you, the best a snook can.' He began scrambling down through the rocks. 'And seeing as you're travelling folk and it's water you're after – I'll take you to the Seven Cooks.'

'Where's the Seven Cooks?' Mog asked.

'Seven Cooks isn't a *where*, stupid. It's a *who*,' Mary sniped.

'Is it?' the snook said, giving her an odd look. 'Quickly now, don't dawdle. Don't stop, don't touch anything, don't *do* anything. Just follow me and keep up. And for Murn's sake, *please* put that book back into your pocket.' He began wading through the long blue grass, heading towards the blue mountain.

'Come on, Mary,' I said.

'Billy, if you think I'm going anywhere with him—'

'Come on.'

'But he keeps spitting at me, he . . . he . . .'

— ELEVEN —

At The Seven Cooks

Wgfn Mgfny was quick and light on his feet,
even through the long grass. So he stayed well
out in front of us. He did stop twice to look
back, as if he was wanting us to catch him up.
But that was just pretend. His eyes looked
straight through us, into the distance, hoping
to catch a glimpse of something else. The
second time he did this I caught his eye, but he
just shuffled himself about inside his clothes,
rolled his tongue around the inside of his
mouth, and kept on pretending. Huh. There
had been more than one pair of legs to that fake
dragon. More than one watcher.

'There's the Seven Cooks,' the snook said at
last, pointing. 'There's your drink of water.'
We'd been walking for yonks, but hadn't got
far. Couldn't have – the blue mountain didn't
look a step closer to us now than it had done
when we set off.

'Where's the Seven Cooks?' Mary said, trying

to be as awkward as possible. 'All I can see is more and more grass.'

But there was something, the smudge of a deeper blue in among the pale blues of the grass. As we got closer I could see that it was a large circle of standing stones. Big boulders really, seven of them. And by the way they all leaned in towards the centre they really could have been seven cooks worrying themselves over a pot of broth.

The moon suddenly appeared right in the middle of the circle, and with it came a piece of the sky. It was a reflection. A reflection in a shallow pool of water.

'Who's for the first drink, then?' the snook said with a chuckle. I was just about to say 'me', when Mary grabbed hold of my arm, and pulled me to a stop.

'Hang on, Billy,' she said, 'one of those rocks just moved.'

'Where? I can't see anything,' I said. But I could. There was an eighth shape in among the standing stones, and it *was* moving.

'It's nearly as big as that phoney dragon,' Mog said.

123

'It had better not be another stupid trick.' Mary scrunched up her face and glared accusingly at Wgfn Mgfny. He glared right back, as though she was plain daft, and spat out a laugh.

'Ha! that's not a trick. You really don't know much about Escareth, do you? That's just Visper. That's just a dragon. A real one.' And the way he said it, anybody would have thought we should have thanked him for it.

The dragon stretched its wings lazily, and with a single hop lifted itself to the top of the largest stone in the circle. There it settled down to watch us.

'Billy – it's a *real* real dragon,' Mary whispered.

'I know.' We weren't walking forward, but we'd started to move again – backwards.

'Well, now what's the matter with you?' Wgfn Mgfny shouted after us. 'I've told you – it's just a dragon.' A look of puzzlement twisted his face. 'What do you think it's going to do, eat you?'

'That's exactly what I think it's going to do!' Mary snapped.

'Ha! Well, it might have done – if half the silly old stories put about were true. No, dragons aren't what they once were. Got themselves a conscience. Took themselves an oath – after seeing the nasty mess the 'Binders made of everything. There's no more laying things to waste, or burning young girls to a frazzle . . . We'll just say our good mornings and go about our business, and he'll go about his. We'll all get on well enough.'

'I don't want to get on well enough,' Mary said, trying to give him one of Mam's blacker than black looks.

'He might even talk to you.'

'I don't want to talk. I don't want to go anywhere near him.'

'Well, you're going to have to – if you really want that drink,' the snook said, rolling his tongue around the inside of his mouth. 'It's his stone circle and it's his water.'

Mary was still glaring at him meaningfully.

'Oh, all right then,' he said, admitting defeat. 'You lot wait here. I'll see what I can do.' He marched off towards the stone circle on his own.

We couldn't hear what was said between Wgfn Mgfny and the dragon. There was a little bit of bowing and scraping (that was the snook), and a little bit of puffing and blowing (that was the dragon). Then the conversation appeared to turn towards us. They both twisted their heads cautiously in our direction, eyeing us up and down with nods and shakes. Wgfn Mgfny seemed to have a lot of explaining to do. And then, at last, the talking was over.

The dragon's wings windmilled the air, his tail lashed out, and with one enormous leap he hurled his huge body into the air. He flew straight up. I've never seen anything move so fast. In a couple of blinks he had disappeared completely.

Wgfn Mgfny waved us on and we hurried after him.

'What happened?' I asked.

'Now that's a real dragon,' he said.

'What on earth did you say to him?'

'Oh, nothing much. He's not a bad fellow is Visper – a vegetarian, you know. No bother at all.'

126

'But he left in a bit of a hurry,' Mog said, curious.

'Ah, yes, well . . .' The snook shuffled about guiltily. 'I might just have mentioned that . . . er . . . Mary's got a bad case of the skin-nibbling snodgrubbers.'

'What's that when it's at home?' I asked, trying really hard not to grin.

'Well, it's a sort of pest. A dragon's flea. At least it would be, if I hadn't just made it up on the spot,' he said, trying to swallow a snigger.

'Oh yes, very funny. I don't think.' Mary's face was daggers drawn. 'You've probably scared the living daylights out of the poor thing.'

'Maybe you'd rather he was scaring the living daylights out of you?' Wgfn Mgfny said.

'At least he's out of the way. And we can have that drink of water now,' I said, hoping that that was the end of it. It wasn't.

'And you're no better than he is, Billy,' Mary said. 'And I'm not drinking that stuff. The water's all murky, and there are bits of things floating around in it.'

'Please yourself,' said the snook. And

127

without waiting for more of her argument, he knelt down at the edge of the pool and began scooping handfuls of water into his mouth. 'The knack's in pretending it's something you really like.' And he added, with his mouth still full, 'Try shutting your eyes if it helps.'

I tried to look interested, dipped a finger into it and, waiting to be poisoned, licked. 'It tastes just like . . . lemonade or, or icecream soda . . .' Quickly I took some more. 'No . . . no, now it's more tomato soupy, or . . .'

'Chicken curry, you mean,' Mary said, laughing self-consciously. It hadn't taken much to get her interested.

'A field mouse with double cream,' said Mog.

'Urgh – no. It's not mouse – it's Yorkshire pudding and gravy.'

'Poached eggs on toast.'

'Fish and chips.'

'A double bubbly and a sherbet fountain.'

'Ha,' the snook laughed, 'you see, it's anything you want it to be. Ha, ha . . . hur—'

His laugh suddenly dissolved into silence.

Something had caught his eye. A new reflection in the surface of the water. He jumped to his feet, and stared up at the sky. Mog's ears pricked and her tail began to flick. She was looking too. I tried to follow their gaze. There was a tiny black dot in the sky. The longer we looked the bigger it got. Then it wasn't one dot at all. It was lots of little dots, and they were all flapping tiny little wings.

'I'll bet it's that dragon – come back to get me! And with the rest of its rotten family by the looks of it,' Mary cried, looking for Wgfn Mgfny to heap the blame on.

'Oh bother!' he said.

'They look more like birds to me,' I said. 'Just a flock of birds. I can hear them squawking.'

They were getting nearer.

'They've got very big bodies for birds,' Mog said, her nose twitching as she sniffed out a scent. 'Don't smell much like birds either. Or dragons, come to that. But I'll tell you what they do smell like . . .' She hesitated. 'Pigs.'

'*Pigs?*'

'Pigs.'

'Pigs can't fly, stupid,' Mary said.

'Oh bother!' the snook said, his usual sicky-green colour turning distinctly mouldy-looking.

'I think Mog's right, you know. They are pigs,' I said. 'Flying pigs. I can see their trotters and they've got snouts and everything.'

'Well, if they're *just* pigs, why don't you tell them a stupid story and scare them all away?' Mary said.

'Oh bother!' Wgfn Mgfny said again. 'You've heard of pig-ignorant haven't you? Well, when the 'Binders disappeared, this daft lot got it into their heads that they should be the ones to protect Escareth.' He shuffled himself around inside his clothes, and ran out of the stone circle, heading back the way we had come. 'Only they've got a funny way of going about it.'

'Come back!' I yelled after him. 'What on earth can flying pigs do that dragons can't?' He was running hard.

'Tin-pot generals!' He yelled back, without turning around. The pigs were getting very close now. The air was full of them, circling high above us. Too many to count. Their cries cracked the sky, raked like fingernails run down a chalkboard.

'I think – I think they're speaking to us,' Mog said, her ears flicking wildly.

'Well, it sounds just like squeak, squeak, grunt, grunt to me,' Mary said.

'No. No, listen, there is something . . . grunt . . . no, Graunt . . . I, Graunt, son of . . .'

'Yes, that's it—'

'I, Graunt, son of Graunt the Magni-*something*, grandson of *someone*, *something* of all the *somethings* . . . *something* High Pigness . . . claim this *something*, *something* of the *somethings*, on pain of *something* . . . er *something* . . . scram the lot of you.' Well, it was a bit like that, anyway.

The flying pigs went quiet for a moment, as if they expected an answer. They didn't get an answer. We'd hardly heard a word they had said.

When nothing else happened the flying pigs began to wheel across the sky in one big flock. They rose and fell with the currents of air. Rose and fell. Rose and fell, rose – and then, on some unheard command, they swooped.

'Miaowwww!' Mog cried out as something hit her across the back, sending her sprawling sideways. And then I felt a sting of pain, and tasted blood as it ran into my mouth from a cut on my head. The rotten pigs were dropping stones on us.

'Billy?'

'Mary!' I pushed her hard against Visper's boulder. Tried to get her out of the line of fire.

I hadn't noticed, but Wgfn Mgfny had stopped running. His hands were clasped to his mouth and he was calling out. Yelling at the top of his voice. But at what? Suddenly the flying pigs were all around him, shoving and stomping, flinging stones.

'No – NO!' I stood helpless. Useless. Too far away to do anything. In the next instant a lumbering scar-faced pig charged me down, and the weight of the blow knocked me off my feet. As I twisted and fell the whole battle seemed to open up around me.

Out among the blue grass the oddest thing had happened. There wasn't just one Wgfn Mgfny now, there were lots – ten, or even twenty.

Of course! The rest of the fake dragon's legs!

Stones were flying all over the place. And not

all of them were coming down. No. There were snooks throwing stones up. Up at the flying pigs.

I could see Mary, standing defiantly, still backed against the largest boulder. Pigs squealing on all sides – teeth nipping and biting. I heard her cry out. Saw the blood. And then I saw Mog – spitting with anger – rearing up at Mary's side. Her claws slashing and tearing where ever they could find a mark.

I lost sight of them all then, as a heavy broad-shouldered sow bashed the wind right out of me. This fight wasn't a match, and it was our side who were losing by a billion miles.

My hands struggled to reach my trouser pocket. I had to use the book. I just had to. If it didn't open up this time . . .

It wasn't there.

Murdle Clay's book wasn't there.

It wasn't in my pocket.

'It's got to be here,' I cried, 'that's where I put it.' But it wasn't. Frantic, I tried other pockets, tried inside my shirt, tried anywhere and everywhere. My fingers dug at the ground, as if I was going to find it buried underneath me. The pigs were closing in again. I couldn't stop them. I couldn't . . .

There was an almighty swoosh of wings and the whole of the sky seemed to darken. And then a growl bigger than thunder drowned out the squeals of the battle. Everything stood still. Fear froze us all solid. The dragon bellowed its fury and for the first time flames roared from its nostrils. It was Visper. Visper – come back to help. My heart thumped, almost leapt out of my mouth as I heard his cries overhead. But then it sank again, lead and ice. I felt sick, deathly sick, all over.

The dragon had flown straight on. He hadn't stopped. He was not going to help. His cries were cries of disapproval, of blame. Not against the flying pigs. Not against us, even. But against the fighting, against the battle itself.

'Wait. Please wait,' I yelled. I could have saved my breath. He was gone.

The flying pigs were coming to themselves, getting ready to attack again. The dragon's fury became mine then. And as the first pig struck – he was an enormous white buck – I flung myself to one side, twisted and turned along his flank, and, as he hurtled past missing his target, I launched myself at him. To my surprise – and worse, to my horror – I suddenly found myself riding on his back. I grabbed for the only thing I could see – his ears – and held on. The pig squealed, rolled, kicked and bucked. I dug my legs deeper into his side, pulled back hard on his ears and refused to let go. His wings beat the air ragged with rage. As he fought his squeals became roars and his roars filthy curses. I didn't understand the words, but I got their meaning all right.

'I'm not letting go of you,' I screamed at him. 'I'm flamin' well not letting go.' I held on.

The flying pig wasn't finished. He beat his wings faster. Using the warm air currents he began to climb, higher and higher, leaving the battle behind us on the ground. I tried to glance down, but quickly looked up again. The standing stones had become pebbles, snooks and flying pigs tiny ants and flies. At last the updraft gave out. We hung there, in the sky, not going up, not going down. Then he folded back his wings, turned somersault, and with one almighty roar dropped like a stone. Breath was snatched away. My stomach was in my mouth. And the world tumbled.

The flying pig wasn't going to pull up. And I wasn't going to let go of him. I wasn't. I was too scared to let go. Too scared even to close my eyes.

We were going to hit the ground.

At the very last moment I felt the tickle of blue grass brushing against my face. And then . . . and then . . .

The world was the right way up again. My stomach was back where it was supposed to be. The pig's curses had turned to wheezy pants for breath, and his wings were beating again, but slowly and easily. He *had* pulled up, turned aside, breaking our fall.

He brought us gently down to the ground, just outside of the stone circle. All around us the battle was over.

– TWELVE –

The Lord of the Pigs

For nearly twenty minutes I was a hero.

Somehow I had managed to win the battle for us single-handed. I hadn't meant to. It was an accident. Just luck.

I scrambled down from the back of the flying pig. He gave me a long wheezy bow, his head very low, his wings spread out on the ground. I think it was his surrender. It must have been, because he followed it with a speech.

'I Graunt, of the house of Graunt (wheeze) – not so young as I used to be – (wheeze) son of Graunt the Magnificent (wheeze), grandson of Graunt . . .' It was a very long, very dull speech, that went on for ever and ever. You know, full up with long endless apologies, pledges of eternal support and that. And somewhere in the middle other flying pigs began joining in, saying their bit, until they were all at it. I tried to look interested. Didn't fidget (much), swallowed yawns, and nodded sensibly when

I thought it would help. Anyway, when the speeches finally ended, Graunt made a wheezy proclamation. There was to be a new Lord High Pig of all Escareth . . . *Me.*

'Er . . . thank you,' I said. (What was I supposed to say?)

There was an outbreak of self-conscious laughing and giggling, like a plug had been pulled. Then there was loud cheering. And everyone was suddenly everyone else's best friend – no matter which side they were on – swopping hugs and telling tales they could brag about. (Huh. If they'd all *really* done what they said they'd done in the battle I don't think it would have been finished yet – and I don't think they would have needed my help at all).

There seemed to be a lot of injuries. I found Mary dabbing water from the Seven Cooks onto cuts on her arms and legs. Mog was limping heroically, showing off the old wound in her side like it was brand new. And Wgfn Mgfny was in among snooks and flying pigs sorting out stone-made welts, bumps and bruises. But worse, much worse than all that . . . everyone was smiling. Smiling at me.

Even Mary, and I can't remember the last time she'd done that without being told to.

My twenty minutes were up. It was time to tell them about the book. That wiped the smiles off their faces. Changed the colour of the snook again too. He didn't say anything, just stood looking at me, going a sort of . . . a sort of colour that doesn't really have a name.

'But you can't possibly have lost the book, Billy,' Mary said. 'A fat lot of use it's going to be finding Murdle Clay if we haven't got his book.' Her eyes searched the ground around me suspiciously, as if I had deliberately thrown it away.

'Well, I have lost it. It was in my trouser pocket and now it's not.'

'Where've you looked for it, then?' she said.

'Everywhere.'

'Well, if you've looked everywhere, why haven't you found it?' Huh! Mary can be a right little smart Alec when she tries.

Just then I felt something snuffling around my ankles. Something trying to get noticed without interrupting. 'Er . . . excuse me, my – my Lord High Pigness.' I looked at Mary first, sure that she was going to snigger, and then I looked down. Standing at my feet was a small pink piglet.

'Um – yes?' It was all too embarrassing this daft High Pigness stuff.

'I, Stod, third daughter of Graunt, of the house of Graunt—'

I interrupted her. 'Yes, well, we don't need to go through all that lot again. Just tell me what it is you want to say.'

'Yes, er, your Billyness . . .' Stod blushed and then went on eagerly. 'I, I think I might have seen what happened to your book – in the middle of the fighting, it was. It . . . it crawled right out of your pocket, your Billyness.'

'It did what?' Mary said.

'At least, that's what it looked like at first. Until I realised that *something* was pulling it out.' She blushed again. 'But, but I couldn't see what was doing the pulling, your Billyness . . . there was nothing there, nothing with a body, that is.' She looked from Mary to me and back again, hopefully.

'Oh yes, and what kind of invisible *something* can just go climbing into his High

Pigness's pocket?' Mary sneered. But her words were hardly out of her mouth before the penny dropped. 'Oh no! It's not them again. Not boodies!' She was glaring at me now. 'Well, the rotten little things haven't been hiding in *my* pockets,' she said, tugging at her dress to prove her point.

I shrugged.

'So – what are you going to do about it?' she asked.

'We . . . *we* are going to find them, that's what,' I said, without thinking.

'But they could be anywhere by now.'

I looked down at Stod, and smiled. 'We're going to find them by air,' I said, still without thinking. 'By flying pig.'

'Billy Tibbet – you are not getting me on one of those things. They, they grunt, and they smell, and . . . and they're *pigs*.'

— THIRTEEN —
The Search Party

It was decided. I was going to fly on Graunt. Wgfn Mgfny and Mog had agreed to share a mount between them, and were going to fly on a stolid silver-backed pig called Squot (Graunt's brother-in-law). And then there was our Mary.

'How do I get onto the daft thing? She won't stand still long enough,' Mary said huffily. 'There's nothing to hold on to, and no proper seat.'

'Just get a hold of Stod's ears. Gently though, like I said – here. No, not like that. *Like this*. You're the wrong way round.'

Stod was trying to be helpful, but the piglet wasn't really big enough for Mary. She had only volunteered to be Mary's mount when nobody else had offered (and after her father had started giving her meaningful sideways glances).

'This is just stupid, Billy, I'll never do it. Arrrgghhh!' Stod shot off into the air, zig-

zagging wildly, with Mary barely clinging on.

'Don't grip so hard, Mary,' I shouted.

Graunt gave a sour wheezy grunt in disapproval. 'Perhaps her Maryness is right. Perhaps she should wait here until our return.'

'Come on, we'd better go and help her.' I pulled back on Graunt's ears and with a steady even wing beat he lifted us into the air.

'Just do what I do,' I shouted after her. She did a double loop and shot past me flying upside down.

'Argh! No! *Billy!*'

'Don't pull so hard. Let Stod do the flying. And remember – left to go left, right to go right. Pull back for up and push forward for down. It's a cinch.'

'OOOOOoooohhHHH!' Mary flew past flying sideways. 'I think I'm getting the hang of it . . .'

'Yes, yes, that's good (wheeze). That's very good, your Maryness,' Graunt said, wanting to believe it. But it wasn't good. It wasn't good at all. It would have to do though, we were running out of time.

'Come on, Mary. We've got to go. We've got

to find those boodies before the moon goes down.'

On flying pigs you can cover a lot of ground. We did. Up and down, backwards and forwards, this way and that way and then this way again before we knew it.

'Nothing,' said Mog. 'Absolutely nothing. And we've been searching for hours.' She was hanging upside down from Wgfn Mgfny's left leg, trying to get a better view of the ground.

'Oh, there's got to be something somewhere,' I said. 'Just keep looking. The book's only small and the boodies are almost invisible – we could easily miss them.' There were several loud grouchy sighs. I should have kept my big mouth shut.

From the air the ground looked a bit like a giant carpet. Where the wind had been blowing it had turned the grass into a pattern of squirls and squiggles. And in thicker knots of colour were the lumps of rock and the dead trees. Only the mountain stood above the carpet, as high as the sky and as far away as ever. That's not counting the moon, of course.

The moon was still there. Just.

'We're never going to find them at this rate, Billy,' Mary said. She was flying on my left – with her eyes closed. (Stod was doing all her looking for her). Mog and the snook were on my right, and they weren't listening. It didn't really matter. All their faces were saying the same thing, and I was beginning to agree with them.

'Just one more sweep,' I said, looking as purposeful as I could manage.

'Down there!' Stod suddenly squeaked. '*Down there!*' Mary got so excited at the outburst she opened her eyes, jumped forward, and pulled too hard on the piglet's ears. They lurched to one side, and fell. Straight down. Behind them the wind snatched half a word and blew it back to us.

'—oodies!'

Graunt and Squot didn't wait to be told, they reared up, kicked back with their wings and dived after them.

'There they are – I can see them your Billyness.'

Mary and Stod had broken their fall just above the ground. A thin wiggly line was drawing itself across the grass plains below them. Or was it being drawn? – by something thin and flimsy, and see-through. Something carrying a book!

'Go for it, Mary,' I cried. 'Go for it!'

We went too. Graunt fixed his target and swooped in low. I let go of his ears, leant over to one side, and stretched out my arm as far as I dared go. I could almost feel the book at my fingertips. If we could just get another wing beat nearer. Just one.

'No – Billy! I've got it.'

'No, no you haven't, I've—'

'Ow!'

Squot charged in, Mog and the snook grasping wildly at thin air. I felt the sting of the thump, turned upside down. Graunt squealed and tried to right himself, only to hit Mary coming across us from the other side. His wings kicked out instinctively, and with a sharp twist of his body he pulled us up and clear. I could still see Squot – Wgfn Mgfny and Mog were still clinging to his back. They were safe. But there was no Mary or Stod. No boodies. And no book either.

'Graunt, we've got to go back down.' I yanked hard at his ears, tried to pull him aside. He wheezed and coughed, and for the only time ever, refused to go. 'Graunt, please . . .' I threw my head back, strained to find them with my eyes.

Below us the weave of the grass carpet was changing, its delicate squirls becoming dirty great flurries, and the lick of the wind a rattle of slaps and smacks.

Wgfn Mgfny suddenly swung Squot across our path, pulling us up hard in mid-air. 'Quickly! We must get out of here. We must,' his voice was urgent, 'there's storms brewing.'

'Storms? But Mary . . .' My eyes began to sting as the wind flung dust into them.

'It's a weather-spell!' Wgfn Mgfny cried. 'We've spooked loose a weather-spell and—' The growl of thunder stole the rest of his words, and streaks of blood-red lightning spilt across the sky. Dust clouds grumbled, turned, tumbled, and deliberately blotted out the moon. And then, like a pair of giant grubby hands, they reached up and grabbed us. Plucked us right out of the air.

147

FOURTEEN

The Stone Forest

I don't remember landing. It was Graunt who turned his body to protect me as the weather-spell hurled us to the ground. Graunt who took the full force of the blow. When I opened my eyes he was right there next to me. Standing sort of funny, stiff and awkward, like he was hurting a lot more than he would admit to. There was blood on his wings, and one hung oddly at his side. Even his face was trying to hide the pain. But it couldn't.

'Graunt?' My throat was dust-cut and very sore.

'Your High Pigness . . . you're alive.'

'Of course *I'm* alive,' I said, 'but you're hurt.'

'I'm not (wheeze) so young as I used to be,' he said, through a thin, pretend smile. He tried to give a stiff little bow, but stopped halfway. And then he changed the subject. 'I've been searching, your Billyness. There is no sign of the snook, or Squot or Mog.'

'And Mary?' I said. I'd almost forgotten about Mary.

His face grew darker and he turned his head away. 'I have found my daughter . . . and her Maryness.'

'What – where? Can you take me to her?' I pulled myself unsteadily to my feet, and as I did I had to pinch myself. Maybe *I* was dead, or still stuck inside a daft dream. I pinched myself again really hard. It hurt. On all sides of us, and as far away as I could see, there were stone pavements. Broken stone columns, shadowy doorways and cracked brickwork around empty windows. It was a sort of ruined city, with roads and walls and . . .

But they weren't the ruins of buildings at all. Not lines of streets, not roads. The stone columns were tree trunks. The broken arches were branches. The pavements woodland streams. It was a stone forest. And what was worse, the ruins of a stone forest.

'H-how?' I stammered.

Graunt didn't answer. Instead he limped forward, led me slowly through a broken stone archway, where one stone tree had crashed and fallen against another. We might have been walking into the remains of a big, open, brickwork courtyard. But we weren't. We had reached the edge of a great stone lake.

There was something lying in the middle of it. Something moving. And something not.

'Mary? Mary, is that you? Are you all right?'

There was no answer. I began to run.

'Mary?' I was more desperate this time.

'She has not moved,' Stod said, in a flat toneless voice. The piglet was sitting quietly, watching over a lifeless crumpled heap.

'Mary? Oh, flippin' heck. Sis – wake up, will you? Please wake up!'

Stod turned her head slowly from Mary to me. I've never seen a sadder face that wasn't crying.

The moon was catching the outline of Mary's shattered body. She looked all done in. Finished.

'Mary? . . .'

'BOO!'

Graunt gave an awkward wheezy squeal, rearing up at the sudden noise. I must have jumped a mile.

150

'BOO!' Mary cried again.'BOO! Lets see how you like it.'

'What—?' Mary was sitting up. And she was laughing. Even Stod had turned her head away as if she had something to hide.

'I said, Billy, didn't I? I said I'd get you back for knocking me out of that tree. HA! And I did an' all.'

'Mary Tibbet. If you ever do such a stupid *stupid* STUPID thing EVER AGAIN . . .' This time I really was going to clobber her. 'I could murder you. We thought you were flippin' well dead.'

'Yes, well. I'm not, am I?'

I can't write down the argument we had then.

Graunt waited patiently until we had finished. 'Er . . . excuse me (wheeze) your Billyness, and your Maryness, it's getting very late, and the boodies . . .'

'Oh!' we answered together, our voices thick with guilt. Then, before we could say anything sensible, Graunt's legs suddenly gave way beneath him, and he dropped awkwardly to the ground.

'Father!' Stod rushed to his side. The old warrior's breath wheezed and gurgled in his throat. His eyes had lost their steel, they were dull and fogged.

'Oh, Graunt, I'm sorry, I, I . . . He's not going to die, is he, Billy?' Mary said, her face twisting into tears.

'I don't know. He's hurt. He's really badly hurt. And all we've been doing is arguing over a load of old tripe. If some daft divvy hadn't been playing silly beggars—' I stopped myself.

With a struggle we managed to pull free the legs that had twisted under him as he fell. Luckily he had fallen against his good wing.

'Come on, Mary, we've got to get that book back. Or, or . . .' I turned to Stod. 'Stay here. Stay with your dad. We'll get help. Those boodies have got to be around here somewhere.'

The moon was very low, almost hidden behind the broken stumps of the stone forest. There was a lot more darkness than there was light. Soon there would be no moon at all. Mary and me tried to stay angry with each other, but it's hard to be annoyed with someone when they're all you've got, and long black shadows are licking your shoes and creeping up your legs. There were no clues as to where we should look. And the broken stones were deliberately mixing with the shadows to make spooks' faces at us.

'Do you think it was ever a real forest?' Mary asked, her voice a tiny whisper. It wasn't a question she wanted answering. It was a truce.

So, I just said, 'Probably – probably magic and that.'

'There's not much sound to it though – I mean, proper sound,' Mary said. I listened. The air was completely still. The stone trees didn't sway or creak or rustle, and there were no birds chirping or small animals moving about. If there were noises at all they were more like, more like . . . memories.

'There's something else that's odd about this forest an' all,' Mary said.

'What's that?'

'Well – if this is a ruined forest, and everything is supposed to be falling down and broken – where are all the bits?'

'The bits?'

'The bits that have dropped off.'

I began to see what she meant. She was right. Where stone branches had cracked or snapped off the trees, there was nothing underneath them. No broken bits loose on the ground. Where whole trees had fallen, only the heaviest pieces of trunk – pieces too big to shift? – were left. The whole forest was done and dusted. Neat, tidy. *Clean*.

'Y'know – the air doesn't smell like a proper forest either.' I sniffed. 'Not a real one. Not even a stone one.' It didn't. But there was the whiff of something in the air. A stink I was sure I knew from somewhere if only I could remember. School science labs or, or—

And then I heard it. As clear as anything.

'Mary – did you hear that?'

'What? I didn't hear anything.'

'SHHHH – listen, will you. There! There it is again. Can't you hear it now?'

'Billy, I can't hear anything except SHHHH, SHHHH.'

But I was sure. There it was again. I'd know

that sound anywhere. I pulled Mary up. Stood her still.

'Don't move. Don't breath. Just listen . . .'

We listened.

Cu-coo, cu-coo.

'A cuckoo. There's a bird singing,' Mary said.

'Don't be daft. Don't you remember anything? It's not a real bird. It's a clock. The Stringers' cuckoo clock. Come on, the sound's coming from over there.'

I pulled her on, tried to break into a run.

'Oowpff . . . ruddy heck.' I bashed my leg, and stumbled over a fallen tree. Or at least I thought I did. It wasn't a tree. But it *was* wood.

Real wood, and not stone.

'Mary, it's, it's the Stringers' dinner table. And a chair. And their fridge. And look, *look*, on that tree – the clock, the cuckoo clock – and, and . . .' And everything else that had once been the pride and joy of number twenty-eight Orchard Views. Beds, cupboards, sofas, a rug with dragons on it, even a shopping bag full of groceries. And there, right in the middle of it all, standing on the Stringers' small hall table, was a bottle of Thornton and Turnbull's Universal Spirit.

'If Aunt Joyce ever gets to see this lot she'll, she'll . . .' It didn't bear thinking about. So I didn't. Sometimes it's better not to.

'Maybe she already has seen it, Billy. I mean, she could be here – Aunt Joyce or, or Aunt Lilly.'

'Aunt Joyce!' I yelled out at the top of my voice. 'Aunt Lilly?' Then Mary joined in. But do you know what was really odd? Our second shout wasn't as loud as the first. Our third was hardly a shout at all. It was as if, in a way, now that we were sure of finding the Stringers, we didn't really want to. They would only barge right in and take over the whole thing. This was our adventure. There was an odd, mixed-up, wistful sort of look on Mary's face. She looked the same way I felt.

'No, they're not here,' I said, still pretending to look.

'But they're bound to come back before it gets really dark.'

'We haven't got time to wait – we have to get help for Graunt,' I said, my face red hot with the half-lie. 'We can leave a note or something, and take some of these groceries with us – so they know we haven't starved to death . . .'

We were wrong. And we both knew we were wrong. We should never have done it. But we did it anyway. There was nothing to write on, and nothing to write with. So, there was no note. I picked up a bag of groceries and, after giving one more feeble shout, we started back the way we had come.

It was then I suddenly realised I was carrying something in both of my hands. In one was the bag of groceries. In the other, to my utter amazement, was a bottle of Thornton and Turnbull's Universal Spirit.

'We can come back for the Stringers in the morning – when it's light,' I said. Guilt piling up on top of guilt.

'Maybe we should have waited, Billy?'

'Well, you can go back if you want. I'm not stopping you,' I said. 'That's if you think you can find your way there on your own.' (That's how things come out when you're feeling guilty). We both glanced quickly behind us.

The legs of the shadows were longer than the trees now. And anyway, was back really back? I mean, one tree was starting to look horribly like the next tree, no matter which side I was looking from.

'Billy?'

'Er . . . we'd better stick to going forwards. Forward's a cinch. I remember that twisted branch over there and, er . . . no, it was just a little to the left.'

'*Billy?*'

'There should be a stone stream somewhere close by – and try keeping the moon on your right hand side, it was on our left when we came the other way.'

'Was it?' Mary snapped. '*I* thought it was behind us – so it should be in front of us now.'

'No . . .'

The moon had fallen so low it was almost impossible to tell exactly where it was. The faint after-glow it left in the sky could have come from anywhere.

'Billy – we're lost, aren't we?' Mary said, in a voice that was just getting ready to heap the blame.

'No. No . . . well. But we've got to keep moving.'

'I don't think I can. Not much further. I keep bumping into things, tripping and *OW* . . .'

'Mary, where are you – have you fallen?' I could hear her breathing heavily somewhere close by. With the darkness closing in around us, a footstep away might as well have been a mile.

'I'm over here, Billy, *over here* – can't you see? There's a light shining through the trees. And I can hear voices.'

For a moment I thought it was just my eyes playing silly tricks on me. But there was a thin finger of light scratching at the darkness.

'I think it's a fire,' Mary said.

'Oh? How can there be a fire in a stone forest?'

'I don't know but there is, it's flickering . . . it might be the Stringers.'

'SSHH! Shush a minute, Mary – it might not be an' all.'

The sound of distant voices was suddenly sharp enough to cut the darkness easier than the firelight. We could even hear what they were saying. Or rather, what they were shouting.

'Smash it up with this,' a thin voice squawked.

'Aye, or this. Hit it with this,' sniggered another. 'If you can't find something bigger to break it open with.'

'Pull it apart. Tear it to shreds – nasty piece of work that it is.'

'Stamp on it. Stomp on it.'

'And stick it in the fire.'

'Aye! Burn it up. Set it ablaze.'

We began to move in the direction of the voices. Towards the source of the fire. There was such a racket going on we didn't have to creep about. Nobody was on guard. Nobody was watching out.

There was no clearing. But just where the stone trees thinned out beside a narrow stone stream someone had set a fire. Its flames licked and spat and scattered an uneven light across the group of heads huddled around it. They were still arguing among themselves, arguing about something they had deliberately thrown onto the fire.

'*Boodies!*' Mary hissed through her teeth. Of course they were boodies. I knew that, from the second I heard their cries in the dark. There were boodies oozing from cracks in the ground. Boodies curled lazily around the branches of stone trees. Boodies carelessly dancing between the fire's flames. Wrapping themselves around the object that was burning.

'The book!' Did I cry out, or was it Mary?

We didn't stop to think it out. Something just snapped. Suddenly we weren't hiding any more.

'I've had enough of this! Enough of this whole rotten adventure!' I was yelling my head off. 'GIVE US THAT BOOK.'

I began to spin the bag of groceries around my head, letting it get higher and higher, and faster and faster. Then I let go. It jumped out of my hand, landed with a thump, and slithered to a stop right in the middle of the boodies. Burst apart.

'CHARGE!' Mary cried. And we did. There was a chorus of jeers from the boodies as we stumbled forward. I was still holding the bottle of Thornton and Turnbull's Universal Spirit. Huh, a fat lot of use that was going to be. I almost slung it away in disgust. But I didn't. Instead, I flipped off the bottle top and squirted.

'A single squirt gets rid of ALL the dirt!' I yelled.

What happened to the boodies then, I mean, what really happened to the boodies then, right there in front of our eyes, I don't think I can say. The Universal Spirit hit them smack on. My hands strangled that bottle, throttled it, and wouldn't let go until it spluttered empty. When it was finished there wasn't a boodie left anywhere. Just stinking pools of sticky black mess, wherever they had been standing.

That's all there was to my part in it. Mary was the real hero. As I squirted the Thornton's she barged right through the squealing boodies, and gave the fire one almighty swipe with her leg. It belched and spat back at her defiantly, but the book shot clear of the flames. I knew that kick of hers would come in for something useful one day . . .

Alone in the stone forest at the darkest part of the night we huddled up close, and watched the last of the fire go out. There was nothing else we could do. We really did want to help Graunt. We did. But it wouldn't be safe to move – not until the moon came up again. Mary cuddled the burnt tatters of Murdle Clay's little book, rocking it gently backwards and forwards, like it was a daft doll or something. I didn't know another thing until I felt Mary shaking me awake.

— FIFTEEN —

Rotten Smells and a Secret Spell

'Billy, it's morning,' Mary said. 'The moon's up.'

'What? Oh, I feel so stiff.' For half a moment I dreamt I was waking up in my own bed at home in Jubilee Crescent. The smell of sausages being cooked in the kitchen was drifting up the stairs. And then my nose caught the *real* stink and I remembered. 'Yuk!' Leathery singey burns, stale Universal Spirit, and boodies – all mashed up together.

'I . . . we've already waited too long,' she said.

I stood up hardly listening, and tried to stamp the sting of cramp out of my legs, tried to ignore the hunger hole in my stomach. Now that the moon was up again the forest was bright and cheerful (well, as bright and cheerful as the ruin of a stone forest ever gets). I could see the track we had strayed away from in the dark, where we had turned one way

164

when we should have turned the other, where we should be going now.

'Come on then, Mary,' I said trying to sound happy about it, even though I didn't feel anything like happy. But Mary didn't move. She just looked at me sort of funny, sort of guiltily. I hadn't seen that look before. I didn't know what it meant.

'What? What's the matter?'

'Billy. You've got to wait for me here.'

'What? Don't be daft. Why should I wait here? And anyway, who says?'

'The book says, Billy. *The book.*'

'Eh? We haven't even opened the book,' I said. 'And look at it – wouldn't do us much good if we did.' Mary was still nursing it like a baby. It was black and charred, and little bits seemed to flake off every time she breathed in.

'Just listen for once, will you? The book opened up in the middle of the night.' She glared at me. Not hopping mad. But serious. And that was worse somehow.

'Oh, ha, ha, very funny . . .' I tried to laugh. But I couldn't. 'And you just didn't bother to wake me up. Well, that's great. Aren't we in enough trouble for you?' Then I tried to glare back at her, and that didn't work either.

'The book . . . it opened up for me. *Just for me,*' she said desperately. 'Oh – I can't really explain. I can't.'

'Well, try.'

'It's . . . it's private,' she said really quietly, as if she was trying to hold herself in. 'I think, I think it was my fault the book got chucked into the fire – or at least, my fault for not getting Graunt help soon enough. When I was mucking about on the stone lake, you know, maybe we missed a chance or, or something.' And then she suddenly burst. 'Oh, I don't know, Billy! But if we ever want to find Murdle Clay I've got to go and help Graunt. And I've got to go on my own. That's how it's got to be done.'

She held the book out as if it should prove something to me. 'I've got to meet someone,' she said, sullenly.

I just stood and looked at her. Lost off completely.

'Meet someone – who? It had better not be the Stringers, because if it is—'

'No. No, of course it isn't . . .' She hesitated. 'It's Idrik Sirk, if you must know.'

'But, but—'

'And I probably shouldn't even be telling you that. The book *said* . . .'

'Oh, the book *said*, the book *said*.'

'Please, Billy, just do it. Just wait here – we're running out of time.'

Somehow I knew I didn't really have a choice. And on top of that – I was being a right silly beggar about the whole thing. 'I don't like it, Mary. I don't like it one tiny little bit,' I said. 'But – but you just be careful, sis . . .'

Mary left me then, walked off into the trees without looking back.

I sat down and waited. Huh, some lark this was turning into. Just sitting waiting while your stupid sister is off doing her own stuff is no adventure at all. Anyway, I started counting stone trees. And I must have got to about fifty million before I happened to look up at the moon. I'll swear it was concentrating so hard on something it was looking at, it had got itself cross-eyed.

The something was just above the top of the

167

trees. Flying low and hard. Searching. I knew them straight away. There was Mog and Wgfn Mgfny riding on the back of Squot. They were leading a whole army of snooks and flying pigs. There were groups searching together. And there were stragglers on their own, zig-zagging excitedly, like mad flies. Turning the main search party this way, or that way.

'Mog – I'm here. I'M DOWN HERE!' They were coming in lower, nearly overhead. 'I'm here, Mog! Look this way.' I was leaping up and down as dippy as a divvy.

I watched Mog lean across Wgfn Mgfny, lowering herself until she was hanging from his leg. Getting the best view. She could have reached down and touched the tips of the trees. Her face looked drawn and anxious. Tired beyond sleep. But I was certain she was looking straight at me. She must have seen me. It was impossible not to.

'Mog? . . . MOG! . . . I'm standing right in front of you.' She didn't see me. She didn't hear me. Nobody did.

Mog cried out our names, and there were tears in her voice. 'Billy . . . Mary . . . Graunt?

Where are you? Where are you?'

Suddenly, they had flown past.

'Come back, will you. Please! *Please!* I am here. I am!'

'Billy – I'm here.' I spun around, startled.

'Mary – er – Stod. No, not you, I mean – Graunt, you're, you're all in one piece.'

Graunt proudly gave a long sweep of his wings and landed. His wounds had gone. Completely gone. In fact, he might never have had them. Stod brought Mary down at her father's side.

'Didn't you see them, Mary?' I said. 'Didn't you?' But she just ignored me, and shuffled herself off Stod's back. It was odd, there was something different about her. Not smug exactly. But something that never ever went away again . . . sort of older, older and that . . .

'I'm sorry you couldn't come, Billy. But well – *I* had to make the triangle.' Mary's eyes were burning with excitement, and she was so full of herself she wasn't going to listen to anything I wanted to say.

'The What?'

'The *secret* triangle, in the forest. And you

169

see, a triangle's only got three sides. I had to be
in the first corner, and the book had to be in
the second, and then when I'd said all the
proper things, which was dead difficult
because they had to be the *exact* words the
book had given me – well, then Idrik Sirk was
in the third corner. So you see, four would have
been too many. Four would have spoilt the
whole spell. You do see don't you, Billy?'

'Yes, bu—'

'After that, Idrik Sirk did all the really hard
magic bits. I just had to stand in the right place.
But I can't blab everything because binding
spells like that are a secret too. They've got to
be kept in the trade, Idrik Sirk said, before he
went back . . . *down there*.' Mary's face got a
bit twisted then. 'He says – he says not to worry
about him though. And it worked Billy. It did
work, and now Graunt's all fixed and well
again.'

Graunt gave another sweeping bow.

I tried to smile. Then I waited for a bit, until I
was sure Mary had really finished.

'So, you didn't see *anything* on your way
back?' I said. 'You really didn't?'

170

They looked at each other, and shook their heads.

At last I could get a word in. I explained about Mog's search party.

Mary was as puzzled as me, but at least she didn't look for bells to pull. It was Graunt who began pacing up and down, his wings twitching uneasily. 'I feared as much (wheeze),' he said, and stopped pacing. 'When we were brought down in the storm – by the weather-spell – down among the ruins of the stone forest (wheeze) – we came down on the wrong side.'

'Wrong side of what?' I said.

'The wrong side of – of everything, your Billyness. It's the spilt magic that does it. When the old spells spring up there's no knowing where it will lead (wheeze). Can't control them at all.'

'I *think* I understand what you mean,' Mary said, still puzzled.

Graunt tried again. 'What we have here is a simple weather-spell. Nothing much to it (wheeze). The stone forest is stuck on the inside of the spell, and everything else is stuck on the outside. And (wheeze), it would appear, whereas we can see out of the forest, nobody on the outside (wheeze) can see in. They'd need a Spellbinder's eyes for that.'

'Huh!' I said.

'One thing's still not right though, is it?' Mary said, turning her head upside down with the effort of thinking. 'If we're on one side of the weather-spell, and everything else is on the other side – where's the spell itself?'

I shrugged.

Graunt nodded to himself. 'That's spells for you. It'll turn up again. Sooner or later, your Maryness.'

'Sooner or later?' Mary huffed a sigh. 'We could be stuck on this side for ever.'

At that moment Stod jumped excitedly and took off into the sky. 'I can see them,' she squeaked with delight. 'They're on their way back – Mog, and Wgfn Mgfny.'

'Billy, what are we going to do?' Mary said. She was still holding the book in her hand. Well, what was left of it, anyway.

'We need that weather-spell,' I said. 'Now – before it's too late for anything.'

She gave me a quizzical look. 'But Billy—'

'Give it here!' I pulled the book out of her hand before she could open her mouth again.

Murdle Clay's little book burst open, and tiny bits of burnt paper spat out all over the place. If there was a wild squiggle scrawled across a blank page it jumped straight off, crashing through the air in swirls of lashing wind and rain that stung my skin red raw. The new weather-spell roared upwards. A trail of thick black tumbling cloud chased after it, stabbing the sky with streaks of lightning as it went. Then I heard Graunt and Mary crying out to me, their voices melting together in the heat of the spell.

'Billy, come on . . . we've got to go . . . your Billyness, jump on (wheeze) . . .'

I nearly did jump. I wanted to. But that's when I remembered. *The Stringers*. The flippin' Stringers. If they really were in the stone forest I couldn't just run off and leave them there. Could I?

'Billy—'

'No. No I can't.'

The weather-spell roared again, snatched

them up and hurled them out into the storm. I turned away, stumbling blindly towards the thick of the forest.

'Aunt Joyce,' I screamed. 'Aunt Lilly!'

The hand that lifted me off the ground didn't belong to the wind. In fact, it wasn't really a hand at all.

'I'm not leaving without them,' I yelled. I didn't care who or what it was that had snatched me. 'I'm telling you, I'm not leaving.' I tried to wriggle free, but the claws around me tightened their grip. The heavy thud of wings beat out against the storm. The huge dragon rose easily into the air.

It was Visper.

'Stop. Put me down. *Put me down.* I want to go back.'

'Yoo hoo, William . . . are you all right down there, *dear*?' That wasn't the answer I was expecting. It wasn't the voice either.

'*Aunt Joyce?*' Aunt Joyce, riding on the back of a dragon?

It only took Visper seconds to fly above the storm, carrying us out into a bright clear morning sky.

The moon was full and beaming. In the distance, and still a head and shoulders above us, I could see the top of the blue mountain – the high peak of Escareth. Below us, and travelling in the same direction, I could just make out an odd bumble of tiny moving specks flying just above the ground. The dragon's shadow skittered across the grass behind them, like it was getting ready to pounce.

Visper swooped.

There was Graunt, in among a crowd of flying pigs. Mary was riding on his back. And close by was the piglet Stod. And there was Mog with Wgfn Mgfny and Squot. Everyone was laughing and shouting, madly waving, cheering us on.

I waved back, but somehow I wasn't really in the mood for cheering. I could feel the weight of Aunt Joyce on the back of Visper, just as if I was carrying her all by myself. The black looks and the lectures to come. The snotty letter to Mam and Dad. The new book of don'ts, and the certain knowledge that somehow the whole rotten mess was going to be my fault. *And*, if it really was Aunt Joyce sitting up there – where was Aunt Lilly? It was all there weighing me down.

The flying pigs landed first. Then with great care, Visper glided in low, gently opened his claws and let me drop to the ground. With a flourish his wings turned a full circle through the air and he perched on top of a large blue rock.

SIXTEEN

Sardine Sandwiches

'We didn't know what to think,' Mog said, purring like a motorbike gone mad. 'We thought we'd lost you for good in that storm.' She snaked herself through Mary's legs. Round the front, round the back and round the front again, before springing into her arms.

'I did warn you about the spilt magic,' Wgfn Mgfny said, his face serious for a moment, his tongue running through his cheek. 'It's not safe. Could have got yourselves killed.' But then he smiled shyly, and began to laugh out loud. And we all laughed with him, laughed until—

Until I glanced up at the dragon. We couldn't put it off for ever. Mary and me. We would have to face her in the end: our Aunt Joyce. Take what was coming.

Aunt Joyce was still sitting on Visper's back, busily whispering into his ear. There was a lot of nodding and winking and good-humoured puffing and blowing.

'You do it, Billy,' Mary said warily. 'That dragon might still think I've got the snodgrubbers.'

'A-hem.' I coughed politely. 'Aunt Joyce, I . . . we, I mean . . .' The whispering continued without a pause. Her technique was as good as any school teacher. She could time her moments to perfection. Kept us dangling on her hook *just* long enough, watching us wriggle and squirm. Until, at exactly the right second, she'd take the strain, and reel us in.

'Aunt Joyce,' I said again, feeling my face turn beetroot. Knowing full well she had heard me the first time and that this was all part of her act.

At last the conversation stopped. She looked up, turned her head towards us and . . . and . . . she smiled. And it was a wide open smile that spread all over her face, reached into her eyes – lit them up – and stayed there. 'Oh, William, there you are, dear. And Mary. And what a pretty little cat.' She slewed to one side, hanging dangerously from Visper's neck in a daft attempt to stroke our Mog. Mary just managed to sidestep her as she fell off the dragon's back.

'Aunt Joyce!'

'Isn't Murn so . . . wonderful,' she said, flinging her arms all over the place. She staggered to her feet.

'What's the matter with her, Billy?' Mary said. 'Is she drunk?'

Maybe this wasn't really Joyce Stringer at all. It was somebody else who just happened to look like her. Somebody wearing her blue cotton overall and with her red rubber gloves sticking out of their pocket.

'The things I've been doing! And oh – the things I've seen. You wouldn't believe me.' She started to laugh out loud. 'Or perhaps you would. I haven't enjoyed myself so much since, well, since . . . well, what the heck, eh?'

Mary and me exchanged glances. Aunt Joyce had finally done it. She'd finally gone completely round the bend. Daft as a divvy. Away with the cuckoos.

'But we have to tell you, have to explain,' Mary said. But Aunt Joyce wasn't listening.

'A forest made of stone!' Aunt Joyce said, her

eyes growing wide. 'Rather messy – but I soon cleaned it up. And magic, the *real* thing don't you know. *And . . .*' she paused conspiratorially, beckoning Mary with a finger, 'a *dragon!*—' Aunt Joyce turned suddenly towards Visper and began clambering up his rock. She grabbed for his tail, missed, and ended up flat out on the ground again. She was still smiling.

The dragon carelessly scratched his ear with the tip of his wing and pretended he hadn't noticed.

'Show her the book,' Wgfn Mgfny said.

'Yes, you've got to get her to listen to you,' Mog added, jumping out of Mary's arms.

'Yes, of course,' I said, and held it up to her face.

'Very nice, dear. Now, would anyone like a sandwich?' Aunt Joyce burst out laughing again, and produced a large bundle of sardine sandwiches from a plastic shopping bag she had pinned to the inside of her overall.

I exploded.

'It's a *special* book, Auntie. It was stolen, and we've got to get it back to Murdle Clay.'

'Yes, then he can put Murn right again, and we can all go home,' said Mary.

'*Look!* It's got a bit burnt, but his name's still on the front. See? Murdle Clay . . . Murdle Clay's Little Book of . . .'

His name – the title – it had disappeared. The funny jumble of marks and squiggles, the stars, the moons and stuff, were fading right off the cover as I looked at it.

'Um . . . er . . .'

'Yes, well, never mind, put it away for now, dear, and come and eat your tea. There's good children.' With that she began handing around sandwiches.

'But Aunt Joyce, it really is a special book. You've got to listen,' Mary spat out, in between mouthfuls of sandwich. 'Oh, it's useless. She's stuck in a stupid dream, and I don't think she's ever coming out of it. Why do grown ups have to be *so* silly?'

'Escareth has that kind of effect on some folk. When they're not used to it,' Wgfn Mgfny said. 'The old spells can go to their heads.'

'Go to their heads? I'll show her,' I said. 'Look! This book only opens up when it really

181

wants to. And when it does, it helps you, it . . .'
She just kept on smiling at us, and took another
bite out of her sandwich. 'Here, Aunt Joyce.' I
wasn't going to give up. 'You try.' I took the
sandwich out of her hand and swopped it for
the book.

'Oh, it is rather burnt, isn't it, dear?' she said,
her words dripping with 'playing pretend'.
'Hmmmmm . . . so it only opens up when it
wants to, does it? Must be a very clever little
book.' She fumbled clumsily with the cover
and a tiny dust storm of blackened paper
fragments floated to the ground.

And then the book fell open.

I could hardly watch. Aunt Joyce became
very intent. Slowly and methodically, she
studied the pages one after another.

'It seems to be showing her an awful lot,'
Mog said.

'Is it words or is it pictures?' Mary asked.

'Well, it's neither dear. It's—' She sighed
gently. 'There's nothing here at all. There's
nothing on any of the pages. They're all blank,
dear. Completely blank.'

'But there must be something. There's

always something,' I cried, pulling the book out of her hands. Well, I could get annoyed if I liked. What difference was it going to make? 'There can't be *nothing*.'

Wgfn Mgfny twitched nervously, his tongue running rings around the inside of his mouth. He was staring at the book, unblinking.

'If it's empty – truly empty – then–' He stopped, not daring to finish.

'What? What if it's empty? What?'

'Then we're too late.'

'Too late for what?' Mary asked.

'But it can't be.' I looked first at Wgfn Mgfny and then at Mary.

'Too late for what, Billy?' Mary repeated, beginning to steam.

'To find Murdle Clay. To find the Spellbinder . . . alive,' said the snook.

'But . . .' In my hands the pages of the book were falling apart. The wind began to catch, flinging small pieces of burnt paper everywhere.

'Oh, come on, Billy – we're not giving up that easy.' Mary was leaping up and down, trying to catch them. And then she screamed.

'EEEEE! Look, Billy. There. Did you see that?'

'What? Where?' I was chasing bits of paper now.

'Can't you see it? On that page. *Writing!* Catch it, quick . . .'

'Where? – I can't see anything.'

'Oh, you must.' She slapped her hands together in mid-air, missed the scrap of paper she was chasing, and sent it fluttering towards me. I stamped my foot down hard.

'There, got it! . . . Huh, well there's nothing on it now. You're just making things up.'

'I'm not, Billy. Honest. It did say something. It did. It said . . . It said . . .'

'Mary?'

'Well, it's just that it sounds a bit daft.'

'MARY!'

'It said . . . I'm up here.'

'What? You are making it up.'

'I'm up here,' Mary said, huffily. 'That *is* what it said.'

'Up here. Up where? What kind of a stupid clue is that?'

I think we both got the answer to that one at exactly the same time. It was one last desperate clue. And there was only ever one kind of up, anywhere in Murn.

'Oh, no . . .'

'The high peak of Escareth,' Wgfn Mgfny said softly, turning a very funny shade of yellow. 'What better place for a Spellbinder to hide than in full view of the whole of Murn.'

'Come on, Billy,' Mary screeched. 'Graunt will help us get there – won't you? And Stod? And . . . and Visper?'

The dragon looked Mary up and down, scratching himself thoughtfully. Then he gave a snort, curled his tail around Aunt Joyce, picked her up, and plonked her down on his back. Aunt Joyce just smiled, and began eating another sandwich.

The snook shuffled himself about inside his clothes, rolled his tongue around the inside of his mouth, and hopped onto Squot's back. 'I'm warning you though, it's a long, long way up.'

Mog jumped up behind him.

SEVENTEEN

The Last Flight

We flew up. Always up. Skywards.

The cold slap of the wind turned my eyes to water. I looked downwards, to where the blue haze of the grass had been the last time I'd looked. Up was much closer than down now. We were travelling fast, without a let up for breath, without a word being spoken. Faces had stopped smiling (all except Aunt Joyce's, of course), and were set grim and worried. Wgfn Mgfny set the pace and it was taking all we had to keep up with him. There was no thought given to the flying pigs who were already falling behind. Mary's piglet, Stod, bravely raised the beat of her wings to keep from losing sight of Squot altogether. Even Graunt was beginning to puff and blow with the effort.

Still upwards.

Only Visper found the journey easy. Always flying a little way apart, as if he was watching over us, his huge wings holding back to match our beat. He never once complained we were travelling too slowly for him.

Still up.

Ahead of us the peak of the blue mountain rose up. The very top of Escareth. The closer we got to it the higher it seemed to get. As if it was forever stretching away from us, trying to keep its secrets to itself. It was a strange puzzle. From the plains below the mountain appeared to have only one peak. But now, close up, it had lots of them. And there was an extra one for every wing beat we took. Each peak hiding behind the next, waiting to pop out with a *boo!* One coaxing us in one direction, the next coaxing us in the opposite direction. And where, moments before, the sky had been clear all the way to the moon, a blanket of cloud – a growing wall – was beginning to form.

'Billy, I don't think I can go on much further,' Mary panted, breathless. 'Not like this.'

Well, there was no more help to be had, not from the book anyway. I'd stuffed the few tats that were left of it inside my shirt. No, this time it was just us.

And what if – what if it was already too late?

We were flying very high up now. I looked back over my shoulder, I wanted to see the ninety-seven mountains of Murn. I wish I hadn't looked. I wish I hadn't. The rich patchwork, the dazzle of colour, I knew it had begun to fade, but now . . . now it was just about gone. A shroud, a heavy muddied shroud curled across the sky, turning the day into night.

Graunt snuffled and grunted good-humouredly. 'Not far to go now, your Billyness (wheeze). Not far now.' I patted the old warrior across his flank. Tried to smile, tried to melt the lump of ice that had settled in my stomach.

Suddenly Wgfn Mgfny gave a loud shriek, and Squot wheeled back on the air snorting and coughing with excitement. Mog dug her claws in for dear life. 'We're here! This is it!' the snook cried.

It wasn't the very top of the mountain, no, just a thin ledge of rock about a thousand feet below the tallest peak. Something was glowing there. In among the vastness of blue rock a pale yellow light flickered, beckoned us on.

'Oh, Billy – at last.' Mary kicked in, and Stod took off, finding an extra length in her stride now that she was sure she could see the end.

Visper gave a roar, and blew out a long plume of flame in red and gold. And he did a double somersault just to show off.

Suddenly it became a race to see who could get there first.

'Last one there's a sissy,' I cried out to Mary as Graunt and me flew past her.

'We'll soon see who's the sissy,' she laughed. I'm sure it was a lucky touch, but just at that moment Visper hurtled by, and as his tail brushed accidentally against her arm, she grabbed hold and shot off with him.

'Yoo hoo,' cried Aunt Joyce merrily.

'Cheat!' I yelled. 'You cheat!' I didn't really mean it, though. It felt so good to play. You know, just for a minute.

Well, a minute was all it lasted. Huh. I might have known.

Our journey was over. The laughter had to stop.

EIGHTEEN

Upon The Heights of Escareth

'Oh no. But it can't be, Billy,' Mary said. 'It can't be. All the way up here just for, just for . . .'

'Smelly Lilly,' I said. I don't know who felt more sick – Mary or me. Wgfn Mgfny shuffled uneasily.

'This is Lilly Stringer. This is just our Aunt Lilly,' I said. 'I *knew* that last bit wasn't a *proper* clue.'

She looked just the same as ever. Her ancient body crumpled up in her ancient armchair, her eyes closed. Fast asleep, right on the edge of a ruddy mountain.

'Is she dead then?' Mary asked.

'Oh, who cares if she is,' I said. If it was possible to take back those words, I would. But that's what I said.

'Give her a poke, Billy – wake her up.' I did, and she stirred without opening her eyes. Her breath was shallow and thin, but at least she was still breathing.

'How on earth are we going to get her down from up here?' Mary said. 'She can hardly walk, never mind fly.'

'We could always give her a push, I suppose,' I said grinning.

We were so wrapped up in the problem of Aunt Lilly that for a very long time we didn't feel the withering ice-cold silence blowing around our ears.

'Er, Billy . . .' Mary started, before her throat dried up.

An odd assortment of faces, caught somewhere between shock and spitting anger, were staring at us in disbelief. Only Aunt Joyce was wearing a smile. Not Visper, not Stod or Squot, not Graunt or Wgfn Mgfny, not even our Mog. If looks could kill, we were dead six times over.

'Oh! You don't mean that . . .'

'No! . . . But, but how? I don't believe it. Murdle Clay's a *he*. A – a man. A *him*. Isn't he?'

'And he's *special*. Not, not a daft old boiler like – like – Aunt Lilly.'

The faces were still staring.

Huh!

Lilly Stringer, our Aunt Lilly from twenty-eight Orchard Views, was Murdle Clay.

Smelly Lilly was the Spellbinder.

'The Twitch, Billy. The Twitch.' Wgfn Mgfny's voice was urgent. 'She must have it. Before it's too late.'

I took what was left of the book out of my shirt and rested it carefully on Aunt Lilly's lap. Then we stood silently and waited.

And waited . . .

And waited . . .

'Are you sure she's not dead, Billy?' Mary whispered.

'SHHHH.'

What exactly we were expecting to happen I don't know. More than what did. Aunt Lilly . . . woke up.

She didn't look any different. She was still very old, her face still buckled up and crumpled like old faces are. Her eyes, deep and black and hollow, still staring right through us. And there was still an odd fuggy sort of smell hanging about her. But . . . but, well, all that didn't seem to matter any more. That was only her on the outside. Like her name – Lilly

Stringer – something familiar put on for our benefit.

Mary was trying to push me forward, so I tried to push her forward. In the end Mog beat us both to it. She slipped in between us, wrapped herself around Aunt Lilly's legs mewing softly as a kitten, before jumping into her lap and settling herself there. Huh, once the traitor, always the traitor. Aunt Lilly chortled to herself and rescued her Twitch from beneath the cat.

Carefully, she ran her fingers lightly over the few scraps of paper that were left, as if to brush away a speck of dirt.

The book suddenly shone like brand new. As easy as that. She opened it up and began to read quietly to herself.

At intervals she would sigh, or smile, or tut, or giggle, or twist her wrinkled face into even deeper wrinkles as she lost herself in its pages. It was as if she was quenching a long-forgotten thirst with her very first drink of water ever.

What she didn't do was take the slightest bit of notice of us.

I began to shuffle a bit. Mary tried scratching

her leg noisily. Playing fidgets.

'You say something to her, Billy,' Mary whispered, without opening her mouth.

'No – you, you're better at this sort of thing,' I whispered back.

'No, I'm not.'

'Yes, you are!'

'Children. What is all the fuss about? Don't you know it's rude to whisper?' The voice was Aunt Lilly's. But it wasn't if you know what I mean. Not a grumbly old woman's voice at all. It was a voice you had to . . . no, *wanted* to listen to.

'Er . . .'

'Come here. Come on. The pair of you.' There was a smile in her voice we didn't really deserve. I just hoped she wasn't going to try to give us a cuddle.

She did.

Sometimes I think I must walk around with my eyes glued shut. Standing close up to her I began to see things. You know, *things*. All around her, sometimes on the ground at her feet, sometimes dashed across her skirt, sometimes on the ancient armchair, and, I'll swear, sometimes in the air itself, there were funny scribbled marks. Graffiti, Mam would have called it. Vandalism, and a bang on the ear, my Nan. There was something very familar about it, too. Like a book I'd once read and forgotten about, until I came across it again stuffed down the back of the settee.

A book – of course. I had seen those marks before. And inside a book. *Murdle Clay's Little Book of Incredibly Useful Words and Pictures*. Aunt Lilly had made those marks. All of them. She'd scratched them out right where she was sitting, any way she could. And then, using up what little strength and power she had left, she'd got those messages to jump right into the book for us.

They were all there. I could read STAIRS UP, STAIRS DOWN on the headrest of the ancient armchair. At her feet there was a map, still with DANGER double underlined. And on the arm of her grubby old blouse, PLEASE RETURN THIS BOOK, AND HELP SAVE. The message stopped, just where she'd run out of sleeve.

Our struggle had been her struggle all this time. What a pair of duck eggs we were. The answer to the whole thing had been right there, sitting at our own breakfast table. Huh!

'Cat got your tongue?' she said. Mog sniggered.

'We . . . we didn't know it was you . . . Murdle Clay and the Twitch and that. We thought you were a *he*, and we, well . . . we just didn't know.'

'I'll tell you a little secret,' she said, her face crinkling into a smile. 'Neither did I. Couldn't remember a thing about it. Not until I found myself sitting on top of this mountain here, in my old armchair.'

'Are you *really* Murdle Clay – a Spellbinder – like Idrik Sirk?' Mary asked.

'SHHHH. Of course she is, stupid,' I said.

Aunt Lilly laughed. 'Oh, Idrik Sirk – gruff as old boots, he is. But his bark's worse than his bite. I was sure you'd get on well with him.'

'He was – he was dead, you know,' Mary said.

'Oh, yes I know. Still, never mind, eh. You can't have everything. And he came good when we needed him.' She gave Mary a sort of knowing quizzical look. Then she laughed again, warming to her subject. 'Now tell me, Billy, how did you get on with the messages I sent you? It was all a bit touch and go getting them out to you. On the verge of snuffing it myself once or twice. Especially at the end! The old boiler's not what she was, eh?'

I sizzled red, but she didn't wait for an answer.

'I wasn't really sure I could still do it. A bit out of practice, I'm afraid. And long distance spells never were my thing. I did try to keep them all short and sweet, especially after my muck-up with the map. Couldn't seem to keep that one under control at all. Maps and geography never were my thing.' She winked at me. 'And as for riddles – I can never think of a word that rhymes. So I don't bother! Ha! Anyway – you got yourselves here in the end, eh? Got the old Twitch back to me, and that's what matters.' At last she stopped. For good, I thought. But no, she jumped eagerly to her feet, flinging Mog aside as she went.

'MMiiaooowW!'

'Tt tt tt . . . Looks like you didn't get here a moment too soon. Tt tt . . . got my work cut out for me here all right. Oh dear me, yes.' In the excitement of finding Aunt Lilly *and* Murdle Clay all in one lump, I'd forgotten all about Murn.

The heights of Escareth were the top of the world. From there we could see the whole of Murn. Not that there was anything very much left to see. The ninety-seven mountains? Nothing more than muddy shadows in a night sky. The moon had given up altogether, and stood so low behind the blue mountain, I was sure it was trying to sneak away.

'Will everything be all right again, now that you're back?' I asked anxiously. 'You see, we've got friends here, and, well . . .'

The flying pigs shuffled self-consciously. Visper twiddled with his ear, and Wgfn Mgfny rolled his tongue through his cheeks.

Aunt Lilly smiled again. 'Well, dear, I'll do my best – but the tighter the cast of the 'Binder's knot, the harder it is to break . . . I'm afraid we mucked up Murn good and proper. It's thoroughly spellbound.' It was her turn to blush.

'Anyway, let's start by throwing some light

on the subject.' She twirled herself around and faced the moon, her fingers shuffling through the pages of the book. 'Now, where has it got itself to . . . ah yes, page two hundred and thirty-seven.' She didn't have to say any daft rhyme, or jig up and down playing hocus pocus. Actually, she didn't have to *do* anything. All a bit unimpressive, really.

The moon blazed across the sky, stopping itself dead right in the middle. And then (a little bit self-consciously I thought), with its best worried look on its face, it began to blow out its silver-white light. As the light spread, the muddied clouds began to tumble and break up, the mutter of thunder chasing after them as they went. Where the clouds had been, the shapes of mountains began to appear. One after another, after another. Still dull greys, or pale washed-out reds, or maybe greens or blues. But better than nothing I suppose.

'Hmmmmm,' said Aunt Lilly. 'Not too good, is it? I really am out of practice.' She shuffled herself down into the ancient armchair and leafed through the book.

There were no silly giggles this time. No

laughing as she read. No furrowed brows or worried looks either. Just plain reading. Real serious stuff. After a very, very long time, she glanced up as if she was checking for something. Did she say something like Grundiggar? Did a distant grey mountain suddenly pop bright green? And did the wind whip up the air for an instant and guffaw with laughter? Maybe . . .

She read on. And she read on.

Did the peak of the blue mountain, Escareth itself, slowly, slowly begin to change – blue here becoming burnished copper there – and did–

HUH!

I'd had enough of all that stuff. Don't get me wrong. I wanted to help save Murn – for the rock trolls, and the flying pigs, for the dragons, for Wgfn Mgfny and the snooks, and oh, for everybody. I really did want their world put right. But, well, it looked as if it was going to take one heck of a long time. If it had all come flooding back in one great big dollop, along with all the usual special effects, you know, like Hollywood, that would have been one thing. But this was looking like a much bigger job altogether. Could have gone on for years. She'd been at it for yonks already and hadn't come anywhere near the really interesting stuff. All she'd managed to do was shift the moon a bit and light up a couple of old mountains. Didn't amount to much at all – not on the Seven Wonders of the World scale of things.

'Er, Aunt Lilly?' I said.

Her head stayed buried in her book.

'AUNT LILLY.'

'What – what is it, dear?' She looked up at me, distracted, her last calculations still written across her face.

'We – Mary and me – we want to go home.'

'Pardon?'

'We want to go home.'

'Oh yes, please,' put in Mary.

'*Home.*' Aunt Lilly used the word as if she didn't quite understand what it meant.

'To Orchard Views. You know, where you live with Aunt Joyce,' I said, looking hopefully across at Aunt Joyce. There wasn't going to be any help from that direction. She had clambered down from Visper's back – still smiling stupidly and with a half-eaten sandwich in her hand – and was now trying to teach Stod how to dance a two-step.

'Orchard Views,' said Aunt Lilly, perplexed. She began to look just a little bit sickly. 'Oh, *Orchard Views*, oh no ... no ...' She tut-tutted thoughtfully. Closed her book, and rested it on her lap.

'Billy, Mary, I *am* home,' she said.

'What! But you and Aunt Joyce are supposed to be looking after us,' Mary cried.

'And we trailed all this way up here to find you,' I said.

'And I hurt all over, and I haven't had a wash for days. Or a proper meal.'

'And Mam and Dad will be back from their holiday soon. What are they going to say?'

'And there's still that rotten Jenny Haniver,' Mary said. 'What are you going to do about her?' Huh, I'd just about forgotten about Jenny Haniver.

'Yes, what *are* you going to do—'

'CHILDREN!' Aunt Lilly boomed out. 'SHUT UP!'

We shut up.

'I'm not going back. And that is that,' she said. Then she added simply, 'But you two are.'

I was about to start up again, but the look she gave me told me she knew exactly what I was going to say, and that I needn't bother.

'There is far too much for me to do here. I can't be bothering with silly little problems like Jenny Haniver. No, oh no, you two will have to take care of her for me.' I might have tried to speak, but I couldn't. Aunt Lilly pointed vaguely at Aunt Joyce. 'And I'll send this silly woman back to you when you're ready for her.'

Well, I remember her opening the little book for the last time. I remember seeing the faces of Visper and Graunt, Stod and Squot. Wgfn Mgfny rolling his tongue around the inside of his mouth. All smiles.

I remember that. And Mog mewing.

'But, but—'

There was no time for proper goodbyes.

NINETEEN

A Really Brilliant Idea

'Oh Billy! I can't see – I can't see anything.'

'Mary?' I stumbled forwards, eyes stung shut. 'Sis – where are you?' It was like a daft game of Blind Man's Buff, only we were both 'it'.

'Ow! – ow, the light's hurtin' my eyes, Billy.'

Light? Yes. A dazzling, fierce light. At the same time the heat of a furnace was melting me. Sweat was running rivers down my face, under my arms, across my back. Sizzling dry, glueing my shirt to my skin.

'Mary – Mary?' I tried to feel for her with my hands. Opened an eye. Snapped it shut again. My hands found themselves against a hard rough surface. It felt warm, and was cut with a zig-zag of running lines. Up and down and side to side.

At last my eyes began to blink open as they became accustomed to the new light. First I took a sneaky look under a shaded hand. Then I opened them full on. There were colours –

blue, and white – a huge, intense white.

It was the sun. The sun big and brilliant in a clear blue summer's sky. After so long with just the moon, it was agony.

'Billy?' Mary was right there next to me, her face twisted tight shut against the unusual light. We were standing with our backs against a high brick wall. A very ordinary brick wall. It belonged to a park. There was ordinary-looking green grass, ordinary-looking trees, ordinary-looking swings and roundabouts, a small ordinary-looking pond, and ordinary-looking litter scattered everywhere. A breeze sprang up for a moment, rippling the water, before running off through the grass rattling tin cans, and tossing rubbish as it went.

'Billy, I think we're back. I think we're home.'

We were back all right.

'Where's Mog?' I asked. 'Where are you, you daft cat?'

'I hope we haven't left her behind,' Mary said.

'Maybe she didn't want to come back.'

Just then there was a very loud, very

awkward, unpractised mew. Mog was sitting uneasily on top of the park wall. She was staring at us, her eyes big and round, and unforgiving.

'Mog – are you OK?'

'Miaaaaaooow,' she spat out, flicking her tail at us.

'Mog?'

'Miaaaaooow,' she said again. Well, she didn't actually say it again, she just mewed. And when she realised she was just mewing, and not speaking words at all, she mewed again.

'Oh Mog, your voice—'

Mog licked herself in embarrassment and jumped down on the far side of the wall.

'Come back here, stupid,' Mary called after her. 'You'll only get yourself lost.'

Mog refused to answer.

'Well, she'll just have to find her own way home,' I said. 'We've got a big enough problem already.'

'Oh Billy, you don't really think *she's* still here? – That Jenny Haniver. What can *we* do against a Boggart-bogey-thingy?' I wish she hadn't asked that.

'How am I supposed to know?' I kicked a crumpled tin can and followed it to the edge of the pond. There was a worried, back-to-front me staring up out of the water.

'It's just not fair,' Mary said, getting huffy. 'We haven't even got the book now. And all she's got to do is look at us and go zonk – then off we go again.'

'Don't start, Mary. I'm trying to think,' I said, only half-listening. I let my foot trail across the surface of the water, and watched as the ripples made the back-to-front me disappear. 'What did you say, Mary – just then?'

'Eh? – Go zonk, you mean?'

'That's it,' I said. 'That's it!' I'd just had a really brilliant idea. 'Come on, there's a gate in the wall . . .'

'I don't believe it,' Mary said.

The iron gate was locked shut. Padlocked and chained. I could easily climb it, so could Mary if she stuffed her dress in her pants. The gate wasn't the problem. But behind the gate—

Behind the gate was a road with a bus stop,

207

and behind the bus stop was a hill. A hill I recognised.

'Where have all the houses gone?'

It wasn't just houses that were missing. The ugly little shops, the people and the traffic, even the muck in the air – they were missing, too. It wasn't that there was nothing left at all, and that made it worse somehow. Here and there, a single red-brick house was still standing. Even the odd full street, left alone on the hillside like a lump of scraggy grass on a playing field where the council's done its couldn't-care-less summer cut. In between the few buildings there was nothing. Just *nothing*. Bare hill.

'What about Orchard Views, Billy?'

I tried to imagine where Orchard Views should have been. I could still remember Dad's instructions. Past the Union Hall, he had said (there was no Union Hall), third street on the left.

'Third street on the left – it's still there!' I said. 'I . . . I think.'

'Can't we just dial 999 or something?' Mary said hopefully. I didn't bother to answer.

We began to climb the hill together.

As we reached the second scatter of houses there was a sudden loud electronic click and a piercing whine that filled my head and shook my teeth loose. 'RRRRR . . . FRRRRR . . . WILL EVRRRRYONE . . . PLZZZZZ . . . STAY WHERE THEY ARRRRRR . . . FZZZZZ . . . DO NOT MRRRRV . . . YOU ARE IN GREAT DANGRRRRRRR . . .' The voice squawked. Loud metallic. As clear as mud.

'Some daft lulu's been let loose with a megaphone,' Mary said.

As the buzzing faded away, another more familiar sound began to take its place.

'Quick. Come on—'

We turned the corner into Orchard Views.

'Oh, Billy. Billy, look at that.'

We'd suddenly found the people. Both ends of the street were jammed solid. Big ugly-looking crowds were jostling and bumping against a barrier that was holding them back. Behind them I could just make out a line of tall blue pointy heads. Like blunt pencils. *Poliss!* Up on roof tops and behind bedroom windows I could see faces and, nuzzled up against the faces, guns.

209

There was another loud electronic click. The metal voice had another go. 'RRRRR . . . FRRRRRR . . . WILL EVERYNNN . . . PLZZZZZZ GET BACK . . . WRRRR GOING TO HAVE ANRRRTHRR GO AT HRRRR . . .'

'Hold that line, Dobson. Keep the beggars back!' A flat blue cap shouted out from behind the poliss line. 'They're going in . . .'

A sudden mumbling hush fell over the crowd, followed by a huge collective gasp, and somebody shouted, 'You'll not see them again.'

'That's twenty-two I make it.'

'Should get the army in on it, that would sort the woman out – that would fix her box of tricks.'

We were still stuck at the very back of the crowd. In front of us a group of men were holding their arms above their heads, click-clicking cameras at the thin air.

'Come on, Mary, give me your hand.' We squeezed past the photographers and between a TV crew who were talking to the bloke from number forty.

'It was brave Spot here who saved your life,

then, Mr Orderly?' asked the serious-faced interviewer.

'Aye lad, aye, it was.' He held up the tiniest scrap of a black mongrel dog. 'He went for her, he did. Aye, just as she . . .'

We slid around a fat couple who were eating sandwiches out of greaseproof paper, drinking tea out of an old army flask, and looking intently through a massive pair of binoculars all at the same time.

That was as far as we got.

'Hoi! Who's doin' all the shovin', then?'

'Find your own flippin' spot.'

'Aye, slippy as fish these two.'

'A right pair of wriggly worms.'

'Well, worm your way in somewhere else. We were here first.'

I would have recognised those voices any-where. Swot, Lippy Jane, Conk and the young 'un – Sprog. The gang. I could have . . . well.

'It's me. *Look,* it's me – Billy,' I said. 'Billy Tibbet.' They looked.

'Eeeee! It is him, you know.' Sprog squealed with excitement, until Swot pulled on her arm and shut her up.

'Keep your flippin' voice down.'

'And this is Mary. This is my sister, Mary,' I said. And then I was whispering too. 'I . . . found her.'

There were far too many how's, where's, when's, and why's to answer. And anyway, what was really going to make any sense? So we just didn't bother.

'SHHHH, Billy,' Swot said, pulling me to one side. Her eyes gave Mary the once over, as if she was something we'd pulled out of the dustbin. Mary gave what she hoped was a thin withering smile in return.

'Poliss have been after you two ever since you got zonked,' Swot said.

'What?'

'Aye – you know – since that Jenny woman disappeared you. Woman's a complete loony. She just about exploded when she realised you'd done off with her book.'

'Aye, had to leg it fast, we did,' put in Lippy Jane.

'If we hadn't gone sprawling, and she hadn't cracked her head against the kitchen wall, we would have been joining you . . . I'll tell you

though – there's been a right riot on ever since.
She's been zonking everything in sight.'

'Left right and centre,' said Sprog.

'It's taken the poliss days to get her pinned
down in your aunt's house. She just keeps on
zonking them every time they go near. They
haven't got a clue – it's great fun!'

Suddenly the crowd fell silent again, gasped
and then roared. 'There goes another four.'

'Must make at least thirty by now,' said Conk.

'Aye, plus three poliss cars, a helicopter, and
the Johnson's pop lorry.'

'That's not counting the buildings and stuff,
of course.'

'Been doin' those at night, she has.'

'There's been talk of bringin' in the United
Nations.'

'State of emergency.'

Swot waited patiently for a gap. 'What are
you going to do about it then, Billy?' she asked.

I looked at Mary.

'Um . . .' She looked back at me blankly, and
then turned and gave Swot another withering
smile.

'We . . . need a mirror, I think,' I said. Then

more confidently, 'Yes, a mirror. A big'un. *And* . . . an old book. It's got to be an old book. A little'un.' There were questions all over the lasses' faces, Mary's included. But they never got asked, which was just as well. Swot gave the nod, and Lippy Jane, Conk and Sprog were off. When they came back ten minutes later Lippy Jane and Conk were carrying something very heavy between them: a large oval mirror set inside a thick gold frame with a metal chain slung from its back.

'We *found* it,' Lippy Jane said vaguely, before anybody could accuse anybody of anything.

'On the wall of the bar at the Pigeon and Whippet,' said Conk. 'Wasn't locked or anything. And the place was empty.'

'And I got this from home,' Sprog said, shoving a small but very new-looking book into my hand. 'It's called *Treasure Island* – me dad says the bloke that wrote it's been dead for yonks. So it must be pretty old. Will it do?' I didn't say anything. It would have to do – once I'd rolled it in the clarts a couple of times.

'Right, then – what's your plan?' Swot asked.

Ah yes, the plan. There should have been a plan. Well, there wasn't. Not a *proper* plan. All I had was my brilliant idea. And the more I thought about it the less brilliant it seemed to get.

'We need a diversion,' I said, trying to sound as if I knew what I was on about. Their ears pricked, and their eyes widened.

'What kind of a diversion?' Sprog asked.

'Something to distract this daft lot.' I motioned generally in the direction of everyone in the street who wasn't us. 'Something that'll give Mary and me a chance to make a break for number twenty-eight.'

For a moment nobody said anything. Swot looked down at her feet and shuffled about uncomfortably. Then she looked me straight in the face. I knew what that look meant. If thirty-odd poliss with guns couldn't shift Jenny Haniver, what was one boy with his kid sister, a book and a ruddy mirror going to do? I stared right back at her. Called her bluff.

She scratched the back of her leg. 'All right. All right – we can do a diversion . . . if *she's* up to it,' Swot said, giving Mary the once-over.

215

TWENTY

The Very Last Bit

The gang slipped quietly out of the crowd.

There wasn't going to be much to Swot's diversion. About as much as there was to my idea, and with about as much chance of working.

'If we hold the mirror between us, we should manage,' I said. 'We've just got to get it as far as the door.'

'Are we supposed to be holding it the wrong way round?' Mary said. 'All anyone else can see is the back.'

'Didn't you listen?' I'd explained it plain enough. 'That's the surprise. Just wait until I say so, and then do exactly what I said. And remember – I'm doing the talking.'

Then we waited. Waited for the gang.

'Just be ready with your bit,' Swot had said, still scratching her leg. 'Because when it starts it'll really start.'

And then – it did.

'Fee fie foe fum . . .' A daft voice sounding just like Conk shouting into the bottom of an old biscuit tin bellowed above the murmur of the crowd.

'Help! Help! She's out. She's out,' I heard Lippy Jane screaming at the top of her voice. The crowd at the far end of the street began to groan, and yelp, and bob about. And then it wasn't a crowd any more. It was a screeching mob. Suddenly, everybody was trying to get away from everybody else, all at the same time.

'Run for it. Run for your lives.'

'Arrrgh – she's got me.'

'Poliss! Where's the ruddy poliss?'

'Mother!'

As the mob swarmed down the street, a weird, awkward-looking figure lurched after them. Seven feet tall, it must have been, including odd bends and twists. Its head was as ugly as a coal sack, and it didn't have a nose or a mouth. Just an eye. One. A horrible great bug eye that plopped and popped about like a potato tied to a piece of string.

To be honest, it didn't look anything like

Jenny Haniver. It did look exactly like a dirty coal sack and a potato.

At that moment a second figure, not quite identical to the first (its potato looked more like a very small turnip), appeared at our end of the street.

'I smell the blood of an English man,' another voice boomed into a biscuit tin. That was it. The crowd scooted. The fat couple with the binoculars dropped their army flask, stuffed the last of their sandwiches into their faces, and they were off! Just behind the TV presenter, Mr Orderly, the blokes with the cameras, and a small black mongrel dog.

'Why don't you shoot the bloody things?' a peaked cap yelled into a radio.

Guns behind windows tracked the moving figures in unison.

'Sorry Guvnor – no clean shot.'

Then, as the crowds dissolved around the Jenny Hanivers, the Jenny Hanivers began to dissolve themselves.

'Must have gone down Bog Row,' Sprog shouted from somewhere.

'Aye, or up the letch and out by the flats,' yelled Conk.

Suddenly there was the gang, all four of them huddled together, yelping and screaming, tears flooding their faces. Really good hysterics.

We'd waited long enough.

'Get ready, Mary!' I said.

The mirror was heavy and awkward to carry. We'd been baby-stepping our way slowly along the street ever since the diversion had started. Nobody was the slightest bit interested in us. We had reached the front door of number twenty-eight. The Stringers' regiment of flowers had been trampled to mush. The front door had been hammered sideways off its hinges, and every window was smashed out. The face of the house was one great big leer. If there had been light behind the windows it could have been a giant turnip lantern.

'Jenny Haniver,' I yelled. 'Jenny Haniver.'

Mary joined in.

'JENNY HANIVER.'

Around us, feet that had been running, voices that had been squealing, and loudspeakers that had been squawking all came to a complete dead stop.

There was no answer.

'JENNY HANIVER.' We yelled again.

'We've got your book,' Mary added, on her own.

There was still no answer.

'It's out here,' I cried. 'If you really want it back, that is.'

And then I heard the crackle of dry-stick breath.

'Billy, *and* Mary. My little darlings,' the voice lied. She was standing in among the thin shadows of the hallway. Almost a shadow herself. *Jenny Haniver.*

'You've come home to me, at last. To your poor aunt,' she lied again. 'I've been so worried.'

I nudged Mary and together we shuffled slowly forwards, our faces fixed with hard plastic grins. I hoped they worked. Our grins were lies too.

'Er. Yes, yes, Aunt Jenny we're home – and we've brought your book with us,' I said, grinning like an idiot. We stopped just before the front door. Just outside of the shadows.

Her thin red eye blinked shut and open again. Her lipless mouth peeled back into its thin crocodile smile. 'Show me,' she said, the smile ready to bite.

'Here it is—' I took one hand off the mirror, pulled the book out of my shirt, and held up the bait. *Treasure Island.*

She didn't stop to look. She pounced. Grabbed the book out of my hand.

'Ha! I've got it. Got it back at last, you stupid child.' Her hands ripped open the covers, and as the spine of the book snapped its pages fell apart. 'What . . . what's this? WHAT'S THIS?' The voice cracked. The eye bounced angrily inside her head, as if it had finally broken loose. She was going to explode.

'Now, Mary! Do it now! DO IT NOW!'

We flipped the mirror over, just as she spoke.

'—!'

Jenny Haniver said just one word. *That* word. That one incredible word.

Did she look into the mirror? Did she see herself there? I don't know. She was gone. That's all I knew. She was gone.

Jenny Haniver was gone.

For ages nobody seemed able to move, or to speak even. Not a scratch, not a whisper. And I thought, maybe that was the end of it. Until Mary said, 'I think it's starting to rain, Billy.'

The sky was empty, bright blue and cloudless.

'What?' I looked up, just in time to see a cuckoo clock flash past me. The clock did a triple twist, gave one last desperate *cu-coo* and disappeared through the broken living-room window of number twenty-eight.

Suddenly there were tables, chairs, beds, and even television sets falling out of the sky. A coffee table, and a chest of drawers, a telephone, a bottle of Thornton and Turnbull's Universal Spirit, and then . . . then, a lamppost. I grabbed hold of Mary and clung on tight. A lorry suddenly plopped out of nowhere and parked itself neatly at the roadside. Then came bricks – piling up one on top of another – then whole houses. Whole streets nearly, crashing back into empty spaces they had once taken up.

Still I clung on to Mary. But, you know, it was

odd, nobody else seemed to be bothered at all. Women with shopping bags were beginning to wander up and down Orchard Views. The bloke from number forty was walking his daft mongrel dog. And as for the poliss – they had done a bunk altogether. Like . . . like nothing had happened, like there was nothing to see.

Well there was. Loads of stuff was raining down, heavy as ever. People, even, floating happily through the air. I saw them. I did.

Then the day suddenly turned into night, and the night back into day again, in one great breath. It was like the whole world had jumped round once. Left me giddy-sick. Then it did it again. And again. And in between the sun shot across the sky with the moon chasing after it.

'Oh, flippin' heck!' I shut my eyes, pretended I couldn't see. It would have to stop sometime.

And then, a voice was calling . . .

When I opened my eyes again, I expected the worst. Orchard Views looked like – well – like a street. No, much better than that. A dull, boring *ordinary* street. And it was all there, nothing missing, just as ugly as ever, except . . . except for number twenty-seven. The big garden wall and the old wooden gate had gone, and the morning sunshine was playing happily against the front of the house.

The Johnson's pop lorry suddenly turned the corner and roared along the road, its horn blaring for customers.

Then the voice was calling again.

'Yoo hoo, William, Mary, didn't you hear me shout? It's lunchtime. I've made you one of my *specials* . . .' Aunt Joyce was standing in the garden of number twenty-eight, surrounded by her regiment of stiff little flowers. 'Come along in now, come along, *dears*. You'll have to be quick, or you'll miss your bus home. And you're expected.'

I didn't speak. Neither did Mary. We couldn't.

I suppose we must have gone in, but if we ate anything I don't remember what it was. And if Aunt Joyce talked to us, I don't remember that either.

The next thing I knew Aunt Joyce was pushing us out of the front door saying, 'Bus *dears*, bus *dears*.'

There were two suitcases standing by the doorstep. And next to them was a tatty old cardboard box with our Mog's head sticking stubbornly out of it.

Mary looked at me.

'Billy, did we . . . did we really . . .'

Then I saw the four lasses hanging around at the top of the street. The small fat round one was waving at us, scratching the back of her leg at the same time.

'Yes, yes we did,' I said. And I added to myself, 'Thank you, Aunt Lilly. Thank you, Murdle Clay.'

I picked up my suitcase, and walked slowly along the street. Well, it had been Mary's stupid idea to bring the cat. She could carry it home again.

'Billy, will you just wait! – Will you just wait for me . . . BILLY TIBBET!'

And that really was the end of it . . . The first time.

THE HOUSE OF BIRDS

Jenny Jones

Ominously overshadowing the village, Pelham Hall stands apart. Strange shrieks are heard from inside its walls.

Masked raiders thunder through the streets on huge black stallions. Their nightly catch is village children.

Harriet, orphaned and abandoned, sees her friends disappear, one by one.

Will she be next . . . ?

Another Hodder Children's book

VOYAGE TO VALHALLA

Robert Swindells

The discovery of a human skeleton in a wood
starts hauntings and hallucinations for Davy.
His attempt to help a cursed viking chief on
his journey to Valhalla leads to great danger
and a shattering climax.

GOBLINS IN THE CASTLE

Bruce Coville

William's used to secrets. *He's* not scared by hidden passages or sinister visitors. It's the usual thing at Toad-in-a-Cage-Castle.

But then the night noises come . . .

Why are they coming from the North Tower? Who is calling out his name? William finds unleashing *this* secret was a big mistake.

Now it's too late – the GOBLINS are out! And they're mad, bad and very, very scary . . .